The Right WRONG NUMBER

KATIE WARREN

WILD ONE PRESS

For information address wildonepress@outlook.com

First Edition

Published by Wild One Press
Cover art by Govina Taylor
Designed by Wild One Press

ISBN: 978-1-959553-06-9 (Trade Paperback)
ASIN: B0BY3HD8Z8 (eBook)

The Right Wrong Number

KATIE WARREN

Sometimes when you get it wrong,

things work out absolutely right.

PRAISE

"Warren's writing will tug at your heartstrings and tickle your funny bone. This book also reinforces that love is love. No judgment is necessary."

- Patty on Goodreads

"This book left me with a ridiculous smile on my face."

- Melinda on Goodreads

"The thing most people don't know about Katie is that she's one of the most positive emotional people on the planet who's been through hell and back. I'm so glad she let us have a peek of that side of her with this adorably honest and beautiful story."

- Dianna Roman, author of *Until I Saw You*

DEDICATION

To my dad—
who always said I should write a book.
Here it is.
Do not read it.

And to my husband—
my biggest cheerleader,
who every time I said I wanted to quit writing this,
he said, "Okay."

JULES

PROLOGUE

Every time you see a funeral in the movies, it's a dreary rainy day, and the wind picks up at just the right time, letting everyone know their loved one is there watching over them. But that's not what James's funeral is like.

No, he had to make sure it was a perfect North Carolina day. Sunny and mild with no humidity and no sudden breeze to tell me he's here, watching over us.

I'm flanked by my best friend Nora and my mother, one on each side of me. They each hold one of my arms, like they're making sure I don't drop to my knees. I'm not sobbing. I'm not upset. I'm not anything. I'm numb. The only thoughts in my mind are that I'm going to have to be the one who picks up the dry cleaning. I'm going to be the one who feeds the evil cat that is Fishsticks. I'll never see the toothpaste James so stubbornly left behind in the sink. Who thinks about toothpaste during a funeral?

Standing at the edge of his grave, my feet sink into the soft earth beneath me. I stare at his closed casket, but all I see is his face dripping blood behind the wheel of his car. All I hear is screeching and honking, the last sounds James heard. Even though I never saw any of it, even though I wasn't even there, my mind makes up what it could have been, what it probably was.

No, I wasn't there to die with him. I was asleep in a dream land, while my husband took his last breath. I was completely unaware that when I woke up my life would never be the same.

Lifting a scoop of dirt in my palms, I shift it around in my hands. Clutching it tightly, I don't want to let it drop. The second this dirt leaves my hands is the second James will cease to exist in any physical sense. Reluctantly, I throw the soil on top of the pile along with a flower. James didn't have a favorite flower, so I picked whatever Nora suggested. Who thought I would be a thirty-six-year-old man picking out flowers for my husband's casket?

When I turn around, Nora and my mother immediately return to my side. Nora's arm wraps around my shoulders while we slowly walk back to the car. I have nothing to say, nothing of value anyway. What do you say when your husband is dead? I mean, did I miss that course in school? It should be a class in college titled, "What to do When Your Spouse Dies", one-oh-fucking-one.

Getting in the car, I slam the door behind me. Nora has a tissue in her hand, tears streaming down her face.

"I'm so sorry, Jules," she whispers. "I'm so, so sorry."

I tune her out, all I can hear are shovels ringing in the distance. Shovels that are slinging dirt onto my husband, so he's never seen again.

CHAPTER 1

Dear Diary,

I may be a simple cat, but I know there are three hundred and sixty-five days in a year. Or is it three hundred and sixty-six? I can never be sure. Cat days are different from human days, as we only mark time by the humans' activities. Days do not matter much to me anymore because I do not care about the humans in my enclosure, in fact, I loathe them.

They are no comparison to the human that used to be mine. My human gave me timely water bowl changes, treats when I meowed in the correct tone, appropriate scritches under my chin at my demand, and most of all, Tuna Tuesdays.

Despite the tragic loss of chin scritches, the sweet talking I deserve, and James' ever-inviting lap to curl up on, my misery does not end there. No. Forget the dire loss of one's loving human!

Universe, how you mock me with the added trials you have hoisted upon my nine lives. Not only have I been feeling unwell, my endless supply of kibble that James used to provide has been sanctioned by the two cruel creatures in my enclosure. To make matters worse, I have not had a Tuna Tuesday in what feels like at least three of my lives. Sanction my kibble if you want, but how dare they take away my Tuna Tuesdays!

I do not know what James ever saw in this Jules. That human's lap is too solid and bony. I find just as much comfort sleeping on the hardwood floor.

Out of pure desperation, I once let him pet me on a Thursday afternoon. He was scritching all the wrong places, and he had the audacity to pat my butt in a very offensive manner. He forced my paw, and I had to get out my scratchers. And for fuck's sake, he is not the only one who's depressed, yet I must remind him every morning to drag himself out of bed just to provide me with the disgusting dietary fare he and that witchy woman he invited to move in insist I survive on. Things in this enclosure have gotten out of paw, I tell you! If I had opposable thumbs, I would call the ASPCA myself. How much is an aged feline supposed to endure?

Oh, James. How could you do this to me?

All I have left of you is my favorite of your socks. I shall keep it close to me at all times, although your scent diminishes with each passing sunset. The humans in this house will not take what I have left of you away from me.

I miss you. Damn it. Now I'm so depressed, I'm even more hungry.

Blast it. Time to wake up my pathetic excuse for a replacement cat dad.

CHAPTER 2

I wake up feeling like my chest was caving in, but that's pretty much the norm now. Breathe in. Breathe out. Breathe in. Breathe out.

I've actually gotten used to having to remind myself to breathe every morning, but this morning it's worse than ever. The grief is still leaking out of me like thick tar. Every day is still a search for how to let it out for fear of drowning in it.

Grabbing my phone off the nightstand, I see it's 7:56 a.m. It's been one year, six hours, and thirteen minutes since I lost James, although sometimes it feels like just yesterday. One year since that phone call that forever changed my life. The phone call that put a gaping hole in my soul, making me never want to leave this bed again.

Rolling over, I stretch my arms over my head and blink my eyes awake, staring at a room that is no longer James', even though his nightstand still contains all his things. The dresser is still full of his clothes. The light blue paint that he picked out is still on the walls. There are so many memories of him here, but not him. It's both a comfort and a horrid tease. A loud growl from the end of the bed interrupts my depressing observations.

Fishsticks is shooting daggers at me like he might kill me at any moment. *Good morning to you too, evil creature.*

Fishsticks was James' cat, and he makes it no secret that he despises me. I'm just his personal can opener who he is plotting to kill. A hateful hiss follows his unholy growl, telling me I need to get up and feed him.

"Fuck off, Fishsticks," I mumble, glaring back. I'm bigger damn it. Not by much, but I'm bigger.

He turns around, flashing me his rotund orange ass. This cat will be the death of me. I swear. Murder by cat. And if I do happen to die of natural causes, I don't even want to think about how disrespectful he'll be to my corpse before anyone finds me. Not that there's ever been much love lost between Fishsticks and I, but after I listened to that coroner on one of my true crime podcasts detail how cats have no shame when it comes to snacking on their owners after their demise, I have watched the beast with an even more suspicious eye. I'd better not die at home or there will be nothing left for my mother to bury as long as Fishsticks is in this apartment.

Horrendous noises from the kitchen make my muscles clench. Sighing, I rub my eyes. She's on perfect schedule, the godawful whirling and grinding echoing down the hallway. For the past year, at 8:00 a.m., I've had to hear that damn blender.

"For the love of all that is holy, will you turn that wretched machine off? Eat something greasy for a change! It sounds like you're drilling a hole into my goddamn brain!" I yell at the top of my lungs.

Wait for it. And...here she comes—Nora and her dramatic stomps in 3....2....1...

"*I'll* tell you what. I'll eat something greasy, if it gets you out of this bed. Get up, wash your ass, and let's go get us some waffles!"

"No," I grunt, covering my face with the pillow. "I'm not in the mood. You know what today is."

My heart feels like it has left my body, and all Nora can think about is waffles? Does she have any decency?

"I've moved into your home and taken care of you for a year. I know you're grieving, but you cannot lie here all day, every day, doing nothing! You think James would want you to live like this? You've barely left this room in a year, and you haven't written a single word since he died. Not. *A. Single. Word.*"

The morning reminder that my corpse will be eaten by Fishsticks one day, the barrage of blender noises like an air raid, and now a painful truth bomb pointing out my lack of productivity. That's it.

"Alright! I'll get some fucking waffles if it makes you shut up," I yell, throwing my covers off and stomping into the bathroom.

She wants waffles? She'll get fucking waffles. I'll even hurry up, shower, and change just to prove I can still function. I might only wash half my ass out of spite.

Nora and I go back to when we were in car seats. She can annoy me to no end with her never-ending antics, her incessant singing, and the weird *Post-it notes* she leaves all over the house. However, rather than treating me like a piece of fine china after James died, she's never been afraid to tell me exactly how she feels. I think everyone needs their own personal Nora—a loud, obnoxious *honesty-button*. By the way we endlessly bicker, someone probably wouldn't guess that I actually am grateful to have her. If it weren't for Nora, I'd be a permanent fixture on my mattress. I'd have perished from bedsores and starvation, and then been devoured by Fishsticks, since it's her personal mission in life to make sure I've gotten up and eaten at least twice a day.

Dragging myself to the bathroom vanity counter, I catch a glimpse of my reflection in the mirror. Wow. I see why Nora's been on my case the past six months. How have I not realized how much I've let myself go? There was no reason to look in the mirror. There was no love of my life to impress anymore.

My shaggy brown hair is starting to curl around my ears in a very un-flattering way. The blue eyes that James loved so much now house large black bags under them. I scrub my face, feeling a beard that was never there when James was alive. Looking down at my bare torso, I see soft skin. My rock-hard abs have officially disappeared.

God, I look like shit. It's time for this beard to go. I look like a caveman.

Walking out to the living room freshly shaved, I bark, "There! My ass is washed. Now let's get some stupid waffles."

Nora taps the toe of one of her red *Converse* shoes against the floor, like she's been waiting all day. She's obviously been up way longer than I have. She already has her cat-eye eyeliner painted on her face and is wearing her signature big curls.

"Holy shit! You shaved the beard! Thank The Lord! You were starting to look like you were a member of the *Duck Dynasty* clan. Also, no offense, but you stunk. I could smell you from the living room. I was considering calling your mother and giving you a shower intervention."

I sulk the whole way to *Waffle House*, arms folded, staring out the window at a neighborhood that holds too many memories of James. It's painful to view the scenery now, but I decide I'll endeavor to do the same at the restaurant in an effort to look occupied, so I don't have to endure the wrath that is Nora. However, just to spite me, she just decides to turn up the radio extremely loud and sing *"Call Me Maybe"* at the top of her lungs.

Her big, curly brown hair flops around as she dances in her seat, smacking me in the face. Her *Go-Kart*-sized *Smart Car* has us shoulder-to-shoulder and my knees against the dashboard. I am so grateful when we get to *Waffle House* that I rip open the door and practically run away from her.

"What? Didn't like my singing, Jules?" She snickers.

I give her my signature *'Nora Death Glare'*. "I hate your singing, and I hate your *Smart Car*," I yell, stomping across the parking lot.

"Don't make fun of my car," she whines, following me.

"I can barely fit in that thing! If a pigeon pooped on it, it would be totaled," I mutter under my breath while opening the restaurant door.

Taking in the smell of burnt coffee and old musty cleaning rags, I moan, "I cannot believe I'm at a *Waffle House* on a Saturday morning, and not hungover. Only hungover people eat at *Waffle House* on Saturday mornings." In the booth next to us, sits a woman with smeared eyeliner, still dressed in her get up from last night. "See!" I point at her, earning me a scowl from the disheveled customer.

Sheesh. You'd think her one-night-stand would have put her in a better mood.

"Do you ever stop griping?" Nora mumbles. Folding her arms on the table, she levels me with a somber expression. "Listen, it's time for us to have a serious discussion about your health."

"Oh God, here we go..."

I've known this was coming by the way she's been on my ass more lately. I deserve and almost appreciate every bit of it, but damned if I want to face it yet.

"I'm serious, Jules. As your friend, I'm concerned. James wouldn't want you to live like this. Being both of your friends, I'm putting my foot up that little ass of yours! It's time," she soothes, reaching for my hand, making my heart fold in on itself. "I know today is the one-year anniversary. It was a tragic accident. We're all suffering in our own ways, but it's time to start living your life again. More importantly, to start working again."

She's right. This past year was nothing but lost time. I didn't know how to fit grief into my everyday life, so I abandoned my everyday life to become a scruffy, stinky, pajama monster. Days turned into weeks, then months, and now a year has gone by and I've made no progress in melding together a world with James into a world without James.

"I know. I'm trying. I promise, I am. James was the love of my life and my inspiration. My life is a disaster without him. I can barely live, let alone write a book!" I groan, putting my head in my hands.

My muse is gone, and I can't get it back. I'll never have it back because James is gone, forever. I have no talent without him. Nothing makes sense without him.

"Okay, let's talk about this. To be honest, you're running out of money."

Wow, she's motivational. Thanks a lot, Nora!

Continuing, she adds, "Moreover, I'm tired of living with a shell of my best friend. So, let's start there and maybe the other stuff will fall into place."

"What do you mean?"

"Do you communicate with him? Like talk to him? Maybe that will help?"

"No. I haven't been communicating with him! He's dead, Nora. Dead."

"Well, I do! Don't sound like it's such an absurd notion. It's been helping me."

"You…talk to James?"

"Yeah." She shrugs like it's perfectly normal to commune with the deceased. "Why don't you try it? You say he was your muse. Well...talk to your muse."

She says it like it's the easiest thing in the world, like I haven't tried everything to make this godawful sorrow deep inside me stop. She says it like it's perfectly normal to talk to someone who can't answer you back.

Finally, the server comes, giving me a reprieve from Nora's bizarre suggestion. What do I expect, for service to be prompt? This is *Waffle House* for God's sake.

"Well, thank God," I say, glancing at her name tag. "*Susieeee.* You've saved the day! We'll both have your biggest stack of greasy waffles and coffee."

Collecting our smudged menus, the server walks away with a nod. Not even a *hello*. Fucking *Waffle House*.

"Maybe I didn't want greasy waffles, Jules," Nora complains.

"Well, too damn bad. You got me out of bed, yelling at me about waffles, so now you're eating them."

"Oh, my gosh. This is what I'm talking about. This pissy attitude. Jules, for the love of all that is holy, you have got to try something. Anything. I'm tired of tearing your ass out of bed every day."

Slumping over the table, I put my head down and sigh. I know she's right. We've always bickered, but it was fun bickering before James died. Now it's just like married-couple-on-the-brink-of-divorce bickering. I'm such a mess, I don't even want to be around myself.

I know James wouldn't want this for me. It's time to get it together, for him. I'll do it for James.

"Okay, I'll try. Anything to get me out of this funk."

At the site of her brow lifting, my ire goes up again. Wow. Her faith is humbling.

"*Yes*," I declare, "believe it or not, I'm tired of stinking up the house. I know I'm impossible to live with right now. You're right. James wouldn't want this for me. I'll try. I promise, I'll try."

We eat our waffles in silence, hearing nothing but the clanging and banging of the cooks and servers working in the background. How on earth do I communicate with someone who isn't here? How can I move on and act like James is still a part of my life when he isn't? Glancing at my phone, I see a string of text messages from my mother. I look up to find Nora scowling at me.

"Yes, Nora. I know what you're thinking. I'll get to those this afternoon. I will."

I've been avoiding my mother, along with everyone else in my life. I promise myself I'll catch up with them all....soon.

"Good, because quite frankly, I'm tired of talking to your overbearing mother."

*****

Flopping onto my bed an hour later, I decide to deal with my mother's texts, for Nora's sake. My mom has been concerned and worried. I get that, but a grown man can only take so much coddling before he goes insane, and now I find out Nora has been having to deal with her this whole time? If Nora's messages from my mom look anything like mine, she's getting at least five a day. I should feel bad for Nora, but I don't. That's what she gets for dragging my ass out of bed for waffles.

Sinking into the fluffy, white down comforter James bought for us, I lean back against the wooden headboard and open my mother's text messages. If it weren't for Nora keeping her at bay, she'd probably have sent out a search party by now.

It's Mom! Do you need me to come over to help with the laundry?

Julian, it's your mother. Just wanted to see if you need any help around the house. I found a girl on the world wide web who is willing to come clean!

Your mother again. I just talked to Nora. She said the sink is leaking. I can find a handyman on that internet thing and send him over to the house.

Julian, it's your mother. I just made a batch of chicken and dumplings. Your favorite.

Just talked to Nora! I'll be over soon! Leave the laundry. You're not separating your whites from your colors. You're going to ruin all your clothes!

I shake my head. Gotta love how she must tell me who she is in every message. Like I don't have my own mother's phone number saved in my phone. Technology obviously isn't her strong suit.

Scrolling through all these texts, I realize how little I've communicated with anyone this past year. I've done a whole lot of nothing. If I do go out, I function on autopilot, watching the people around me and attempting to imitate them so I look like a functioning human being. When I wasn't pretending, I was sulking. I've been a bad friend, a bad son, a bad writer, and a bad cat dad. It's not like Fishsticks even likes me to begin with, but still.

I sigh and start replying to the string of text messages.

JULES: Hey Mom. How have you been doing?

MOM: Have you eaten?

ME: Yes, I've eaten! I went out with Nora this morning for waffles.

MOM: Oh, good. I was worried you weren't eating. I can come over. I can cook dinner tonight.

Oh, God no. I can't deal with my mother right now. I love her to death, but she can be a little, well, much. I need to be on my A-Game if I see her face-to-face, but hey, I did wash my ass today. Or…half of it.

ME: No, Ma. I'm thinking of going out to dinner tonight. Get a change of scenery. Next time I need food, I'll be sure to call.

It's just a little white lie. A harmless lie never hurt anyone.

MOM: Okay hun. You just say the word, and I'll bring lasagna.

Phew, crisis averted. Mission complete. Mom—officially handled. Of course, she feels the need to force feed me, doing what she does best. Now to the next matter at hand.

How do I get my muse back? How do I get my muse back when my muse is dead? I know he's up there looking down, shaking his finger at me, telling me to get my ass in gear. He was always good at that when I couldn't get through my writer's blocks. I could usually finish a book by my deadlines with no issue, but now I can't even get my ass to sit in front of the computer.

I scroll through my phone mindlessly, running through my missed call log. I gave up long ago trying to answer them all. There were too many sad voices. Fellow authors, James' friends, and people I've hardly ever spoken to. James' family was the hardest to hear. I finally turned off the volume and let them all go straight to voicemail.

Skimming through my voicemail box, I hit *Delete All.* I don't even need to listen to the messages. I know what they say. Just mournful remarks about how everyone feels so bad for me. Deleted.

There. Now my voicemail is back up and running. One more step toward adulthood.

Checking my missed call log, James' name stares back at me. My finger is frozen in midair. Fuck. Slouching against my headboard, tears immediately pool in my eyes.

He called that night before he left his business meeting, probably to tell me he was on his way home. I was asleep. I missed the call, and that will haunt me for the rest of my life. A queasy feeling sets into my stomach, knowing I missed that chance.

I click on his name anyway and stare at it. I'll never see his name pop up on my phone again. I'll never see another call come through or see a text from him on my screen again. My thumb hovers over the reply button.

Nora says to communicate with him, to talk to him. Maybe this is how. It's the only way that feels real. I'll write out my feelings by texting him again.

Except I don't know what to say. I type. I delete, and I retype. I repeat the cycle again and again. I can't decide what to say. What do you say via text to your dead husband?

I miss you. I miss you so damn much it hurts.

There. That pretty much sums it up. Hitting send, I shake my head.

This is ridiculous. It's not like he's going to text me back. Why am I putting myself through this? Nora says it helps her to talk to him? Well, good for Nora, but Nora thinks green smoothies that taste like grass help, but they do not. I know from experience.

I did well today, lots of adulting. Waffles, my mom, and Nora. I think that merits a nap. Rolling over, I inhale the pillow that no longer smells like James.

"Noraaa! Don't bother me for at least an hour! I'm taking my afternoon nap!"

I can hear her sigh from down the hall. "You get *one hour!* Then I want you up for dinner and movie night. I picked an eighties flick for this week's selection!"

Oh, fucking hell—movie night. And I thought today couldn't get any worse.

CHAPTER 3

"Yo! Liam! Lunchtime. Let's roll!" Oscar wails from his office next door.

"Yeah, I'm coming!" I yell back, running my hands through my overgrown blonde hair.

I'll have to make a point to get to the barber this week and get a trim. Life has been way too busy between work and Oscar hauling me out to the bar every other night. I need a damn break. I'm getting too old for this shit. Being in your thirties makes Oscar's bar nights much harder to bounce back from.

I walk out of my office, meeting Oscar in the hall. He looks like his normal ridiculous self today in his knockoff suit and overly gelled hair. I swear he puts so much product in that hair, I could bounce a quarter off it.

"Where are we headed?" I ask. "Before you answer that, *no*. I'm sick of *Hooters*. The wings just aren't that great, man."

"We don't go there for the wings!" he argues.

"Oh, shut up. Let's just go to the diner down the street."

I'm fully aware that Oscar does not go to *Hooters* for the food. He goes for the '*fine ass waitresses.*' One more thing I need to add to my getting-too-old-for-this-shit list.

The diner is within walking distance of our office. Walking downtown and taking in the historic buildings gives me a much-needed reprieve from the stuffy building where we spend ten hours a day.

Glancing over, I notice Oscar scowling. I know it's because he won't get to see his normal *Hooters* waitress today. No doubt he'll moan and complain about it the entire time through lunch. Honestly, I'm only friends with him because we're forced to spend our long workday together. He's grown on me. Like an inoperable tumor.

Sliding into a booth at the diner, I pull my new phone out of my pocket to plug in the few contacts that I want to add in it. I needed an upgrade and decided to get a new phone number to boot. I swear, by lunchtime every day I had at least three text messages asking me if I was busy that night. I'm not a perfect man by any stretch of the imagination, but I need to get my life on track. Hooking up with random women just isn't doing it for me anymore. I mean, isn't thirty-six a little old to be a barfly?

"Wow. Look at that fancy ass new phone. What? Did your old one take a shit from all the porn on it?" Oscar asks with a smirk.

"Shut up. I got an upgrade. What's your number?" I ask, changing the subject.

I don't need Oscar up my ass about my life. He wouldn't even consider getting a new phone number. He couldn't bear the thought of losing a potential hook-up. Honestly, the less he knows about my life the better.

Glancing at the phone, I notice the words *NEW MESSAGE* pop up on the notifications list. Swiping the screen, I see a message from an unknown number.

I miss you. I miss you so damn much it hurts.

Someone...misses me? I don't know who this is, and I don't know anyone who would miss me but my mom. My heart sinks inside my chest. That's just kind of sad.

Looking at it quizzically, I flip the phone screen toward Oscar, so he can read it. "Do you know this number from the bar?" I ask, pointing to the top of the screen.

Squinting at the phone, he shakes his head. "Nope. Who is it?"

"No clue," I answer, shaking my head.

"Damn, bro. Someone *misses* you? You're not supposed to be so good that they miss you. You can't play the field and be missed at the same time. Have I taught you nothing?"

I mentally run down a list of all my one-night stands from the past year. I haven't hooked up with anyone who would send this type of text. The only texts I would be getting from them is a 'Are you free tonight?'

Shit. Could it be that woman from a few weeks ago? She seemed a little clingy. She wouldn't have my new number though. No. This text can't be meant for me.

This is exactly why I changed my number, to get away from texts like these. I got a new number and now I'm getting text from another version of me. Some pathetic thirty-six-year-old flooded by one-night stands that don't scratch the surface.

"Well, she obviously misses you *so damn much,*" Oscar says, chuckling.

I consider this for a minute before I'm interrupted by our server. We place our orders, and I'm back to staring at my phone.

"No, no way. I have no idea who this is," I say, shaking my head. "I haven't given my new number out to anyone but my mom, you, and a few relatives."

"Oh, just text it back and find out who misses you *so damn much* already. I'm officially invested."

Of course, Oscar is invested. He doesn't have a life of his own, so he's got to be all up in mine.

"Someone probably just texting the wrong number. They'll figure it out eventually," I say, pocketing the phone.

"Alright. Bar tonight after work? I need a drink. It's been a long week."

I shake my head. "Dude, it's only Monday."

I'm secretly getting tired of Oscar and his bar scenes. Even though he would give me shit if he knew, sometimes I just want a night at home watching cheesy movies on the couch with someone who compliments me, like my mom and dad used to do.

My mom and dad were the epitome of kindred spirits, and even though my dad died too young, I realize now how lucky they were to have what they had while they had it. My childhood was full of catching them exchanging sloppy kisses and dancing in the kitchen. They were the lucky ones.

Where did I get so off track? Awkward mornings, meaningless hook-ups, and work. Wash, rinse, repeat. After we finish eating, I get up from the booth, throwing down the tip that Oscar always skimps on.

"Come on dude, back to the grind." I sigh.

Time to get back to my tedious job with my obnoxious friend. Such is life.

*****

I've been staring at this computer screen way too long. All the streams of code on my screen are starting to blur into one. I shouldn't be working from home, I put in enough hours at the office, but it's not like I have anything better to do with my time these days. Sitting back in my office chair, I take in the surroundings of my sad bachelor pad apartment.

The walls are plain white and adorned with nothing of sentimental value. The furnishings are sparse with just the bare necessities and the refrigerator holds only condiments. This place is pitiful and needs an interior decorator. But it's not like anyone comes here when it's light outside. When women come over, I don't even have to turn on the light. Aside from those visitors, my social life is pretty much zero.

Shutting my laptop, I rub my temples. I've been so wrapped up with work these past two days I've had hardly any time to check my phone. Snatching it out of the desk drawer, I see one lonely text. Running my finger across the notification bar, I notice it's from the same unknown number I got that cryptic text from a few days ago.

I miss your smell. I miss your laugh. I miss your everything.

I stiffen in my chair, my hand splaying across my chest at the thought of someone missing me. I immediately snap out of it, remembering this text isn't for me. It's for someone else, but God, it makes me realize how much I would love to be missed like this.

Who the hell is this person? Who do they miss this much? It's got to be someone's ex-girlfriend. I mean it could be an ex-boyfriend, but I know damn well Oscar would never say anything like this to a woman. This sounds like how my mom would sound. She always said how much she missed my dad's scent. This sounds like a woman in love.

They must have changed their number, and I got their old one. They recycle numbers, don't they? That's got to be it.

I wonder if she's hot? Man, I obviously need to get laid if I'm wondering whether a random text message has a hot girl behind it. I slam my phone down, opening my laptop to stare at more streams of code. I try to focus my eyes, zooming in on the random letters in front of me. My mind keeps drifting off, thinking about how much my mom loved the way my father smelled. Lifting the collar of my shirt, I give it a whiff, smelling just a trace of my cologne leftover from this morning. Has anyone ever missed my smell? What I would give to have a relationship like my mom and dad did, to have a woman smell my pulse point and sigh.

Looking down at my lap, I notice I'm already sporting a semi. Just the thought of a woman smelling my neck and liking my smell has me turned on. Great, guess I'm rubbing one out tonight. Remembering Oscar's offer from earlier, I realize there are worse things than rubbing one out at home alone. I could be stuck at the bar with Oscar.

CHAPTER 4

I've been conned into a dinner with Nora...and my mother. As much as I try not to have Nora and my mother in the same room, it happens more frequently than I'd like to admit. Fishsticks hisses at me from beneath the table. I'm being summoned to feed him.

"Nora, I think Fishsticks is hungry. He's hissing at me again," I inform her with a shudder. I glance away from him, trying not to make eye contact.

Nora huffs, "No, he's not! I just fed his fat ass. He's trying to trick you into a second meal. Don't fall for it. Stay strong."

"Come on. Just feed him so he stops looking at me like that," I say, getting a glimpse of his perpetually perturbed green eyes, the eyes that are currently sending a signal that he definitely will kill me in my sleep. "Please, make him stop," I whisper.

"He's mad because I've put him on a diet. He weighs twenty-three pounds! James obviously fed him whatever he wanted. I mean, look at him!" Nora says, gesturing to Fishsticks.

"Damn right he did! He loved that evil cat! He had a whole stash of treats up in the cabinet for him. Fishsticks learned how to break into it. It was a nightmare," I explain.

At the word treats, Fishsticks leaps onto the counter underneath the cabinet where his treats used to be, growling in my face like he's mad that his snacks are gone. If a cat were able to give you the stink eye, this look would be it.

"He likes you more than he likes me. Do something with him," I say, pointing at Fishsticks like he's an object because how can you sympathize with something so hostile? "Take it away, Nora."

"He doesn't like me. He just tolerates me. Fishsticks only liked one person, and that was James," she says, grunting as she picks up all twenty-three pounds of Fishsticks. She sets him on the floor gently, shooing him out of the kitchen. He slugs off in slow motion with his sock in his mouth. God, that fucking sock.

My mom starts in as soon as she pulls the lasagna out of the oven. "So, honey, how have you been doing? Nora tells me you're back at the gym. That's so good to hear!"

Sitting down at our small dining room table, I give Nora the side eye. "Yes. Nora may have gotten me back to the gym, but she has yet to conquer the feat of the grass smoothie."

Nora snickers beside me. "You should have seen him when he had his first one. You'd think the world was ending with all the gagging he did."

"It tasted like dirt, and I couldn't stop pooping for a week!" I retort.

"Julian Alan! We are *eating* here! We don't need to know about your bowel movements," Mom shouts, shoving her blonde hair over her shoulder.

Yeah, she can say that, but she's not the one who had explosive diarrhea for a full week. I'll never touch a smoothie that is the color green again. The whole situation was traumatizing.

"It's time to get serious, we all need to talk," Nora adds.

I know what she's up to.

"Let's not. Please."

"So Julian, how is your writing coming along?" My mother says in her best nagging voice.

I know that tone all too well. I've heard it my whole life. I heard it every time she wanted me to clean my room. Every time she wanted me to finish my homework at the kitchen table. And that one time I brought home a boy that had his nose pierced.

"It's going well, actually. I got a chapter done the other day, so I'm getting my groove back. Now I just need some inspiration."

I'm lying through my teeth. I got two sentences done after staring at the computer for an hour, but no one needs to know that. No one needs to know that I'm a sorry excuse for a writer.

"Oh, honey, I know. It's been over a year now. Have you thought about seeing someone new? Getting on that app with the swipes maybe? You know James would want nothing more than for you to be happy," my mother suggests.

"*Tinder?* Ma!" I yell while Nora chuckles beside me, going into a full-on belly laugh. How on earth does my mother know about *Tinder?*

"Yes, that's it! *The Tinder!*" My mother exclaims.

"If Jules would be on anything it would be *Grindr,*" Nora says, while tears stream down her face.

I give her a pointed stare. This can't be real life.

"If I meet someone, it is NOT going to be on *Tinder*...or *Grindr.* Thank you for pointing that one out, Nora," I snap.

After my mom leaves and the insufferable dinner is over, I shuffle back to my room. There's only so much henpecking I can take in one day, and I've officially hit my limit.

Yanking out my phone, I decide to tell James all about this night of horrors. He would have loved this.

> **My mom came over for dinner. It was sadistic. Nora laughed her ass off. You would have loved it. Mom tried to get me on "The Tinder". She misses you, by the way.**
>
> **I should add, though, that you don't need to worry. I'm not desperate enough for The Tinder.**

I will never join *Tinder*. If I meet someone, it'll be the old-fashioned way. At a bar or something, like a normal person. You know, let the universe work its magic or whatever. I'll know when I'm ready to start dating again. Um, I mean when I decide to leave the house again.

CHAPTER 5

I finally relented and went out to the bar with Oscar. And although I will admit that I need a good lay as much as the next guy, I'm over this scene. Oscar, however, is fucking relentless.

Mixers reeks of spilled beer and hopelessness. The ugly wood paneling on the walls with neon beer signs and the dim lighting that makes everyone look more attractive than they really are just makes me cringe. The jukebox plays some sad songs about heartbreak, probably picked by a girl on the rebound looking for a good time. Oscar acts like this bar is full of opportunities. It's not. It's full of people thinking of one thing—sex. I'm just not in the mood for meaningless sex tonight. Frankly, I'm tired of anything without meaning. I want something real. I want a real life.

"What about her?" Oscar whispers to me above his beer.

Glancing over, I find a cute blonde in a skimpy outfit. "I don't know. She's alright." I shrug.

"What's your deal man? Are you not down for some nookie tonight or what?"

Nookie? I swear, all Oscar thinks about is sex and he has the vocabulary of a frat boy.

"Why are you so concerned about my sex life? I'm fine. I'm just not feeling this tonight, that's all," I mutter, taking a swig of my beer.

"You have half of the girls at this bar looking at you and you're *not feeling it*? With that dirty blonde hair, those deep brown eyes, and that badass tattoo you hide, you could have any girl in here, yet you're acting like you could care less. Honestly, I'm kind of jealous of you right now."

"Oh, look. That girl at two o'clock is giving you the sexy eyes," I say, leaning in his direction.

Not really, but he doesn't need to know that. I just need him off my back. He's like a puppy, easily distracted.

Oscar looks over his shoulder. "Her? The girl in the blue? I think she's looking at you, bro."

My phone lets off a series of dings from my pocket, saving me from my lie. Pulling it out, I check the series of messages.

My mom came over for dinner. It was sadistic. Nora laughed her ass off. You would have loved it. Mom tried to get me on "*The Tinder*". She misses you, by the way.

I should add, you don't need to worry. I'm not desperate enough for *The Tinder*.

I don't know anyone named Nora, and I don't know anything about someone's mother wanting them to join *Tinder*.

Oscar peers over my shoulder. "Dude, is that the I-miss-you-so-damn-much girl?"

"Yeah. Weird right?" I shrug nonchalantly, putting the phone back in my pocket.

"Text her back! She's obviously single and needs a hook-up just as bad as your cranky ass. Look, her mother even suggested *Tinder*!" Oscar yells a little too loudly into my ear.

"Really, Oscar? This girl obviously thinks I'm someone else. You're such a dumbass sometimes." I sigh, shaking my head.

Oscar holds up his hands at me. "Just giving my bro a few suggestions. That's all, but I do think you should text her back. I want to know all the details too," he says with a smirk.

Getting up off my creaky barstool, I gulp down the rest of my beer. "I'm out of here. I've had enough for tonight, and I've got an early meeting tomorrow."

A sorry excuse, but whatever. Freedom is only a few paces away.

As I'm walking out the door, I hear Oscar yell from across the bar, "Text her back! Jump on that rebound booty while you still have a chance!"

I glance back at him and shake my head. Sometimes I don't know why I'm even friends with him.

I take the long way back to my apartment, pondering what my life has become. A boring job, a single life, and an obnoxious friend. I wonder if Oscar is right, and I am changing. I'm not feeling this hookup thing anymore. It never leads anywhere, and each time I regret it more than the last. One-night stands are fun and all, but I'm just as lonely with them as I am without them.

CHAPTER 6

Now that I'm back on my gym routine with Nora, I'm to be up at 7:00 a.m. every morning to '*get your abs back.*' I'll do the gym thing, but I draw the line at the smoothie she tried to shove in my face this morning. She'll never give up, but I'll never give in.

Stomping my feet on the treadmill in this fancy gym has ended up being quite invigorating. It's the perfect way to work out some of my emotions. Even though I miss James every damn day, Nora is right—this is good for me. It reminds me of the times when James and I ran on these treadmills twice a week. We would work out in tandem, panting and sweating together. I prefer working out with James because I could stare at his ass the entire time, but Nora's company is okay too. I guess.

Huffing and puffing on the treadmill next to me, she yells over her earbuds, "Talking to James yet?"

"No," I gasp, out of breath.

"*What?*" she shrieks at me.

She could hear me if she took off her damn earbuds.

"I said I'm working on it!" I yell louder, making the whole gym look in our direction.

She nods, turning her treadmill up a notch. I don't even think she heard me. I shrug my shoulders and bend my head down to keep my pace.

Yeah, I tell myself. I'm working on it. Getting my life back together hasn't been the easiest, but I'm tired of everyone else walking on egg-shells around me. Nora's the only one who is willing to put my ass into gear, and as annoying as she can be, she's my best friend who has my best interests at heart.

I remember the time in second grade when she shoved me down the big slide on the school playground that I was so scared to go down. After that, I went down that slide a hundred times, having the best time of my second-grade life. That's what Nora does best. She shoves you around because she knows it's good for you.

After I take a long, hot gym shower, Nora decides to go home and feed the furry demon while I wander around downtown. I need fresh air and a change of scenery. James and I used to love walking hand in hand down here, just moseying around and looking at all the cute shops. We always stayed on the historical side of downtown, where the farmer's market would be set up with little craft booths and fresh produce stands.

Swinging the door of our favorite coffee shop open, I walk into *The Cup Connection*. We always loved how they serve their coffee in vintage teacups, probably all found at the little secondhand shop across the street. *The Cup Connection* is small, painted bright purple, and full of paintings by local artists. We used to sit here for hours while I worked on my computer, and he'd sit next to me reading a book. The comfortable silences were one of the things that made our relationship great. Sometimes, it's in the silence where you learn about someone the most.

I sit down in our usual spot with my little teacup of cappuccino. Our table has a big aloe plant in the middle that James and I named *Allie the Aloe*. I give the aloe plant a little tap. She's grown a lot since the last time I was here. I'm glad she's been taken care of without me.

I pull my phone out of my pocket, setting it on the table. I've text-ed James twice already. I'm not expecting a response from a dead man obviously, but I do have to admit that I like pretending that I'm talking to him. I like being able to communicate about how much I miss him, about how big our love was. I'll give this one to Nora, she was right. It really does help.

Looking around the coffee shop and seeing all these people talking during lunch makes me feel reminiscent. I find the string of text messages I've sent him and type a new one out.

I'm at *The Cup Connection*. Remember when we used to sit here and talk about our days? Every Sunday morning at 11, we'd sit here, talking about our week. Talking about our big plans for the week to come. And sometimes, we'd say nothing. It was one my favorite parts about being with you, sitting with the silence.

There's too much silence now without you. Big pockets of it that are impossible for me to fill up.

Remember how we always used to veg out on the couch in our underwear and watch movies all night? Now I'm stuck with Nora and her sarcastic commentary. We watched *The Breakfast Club* the other night. It wasn't the same without you. Your absence isn't quiet. Sometimes it's the loudest thing on earth. It weighs down on me so heavily that it makes it impossible to breathe.

Setting my phone down, I look around the coffee shop. My eyes draw to a man by himself in the opposite corner, looking at his phone with an apprehensive expression. He looks up, his deep-set blue eyes darting around the room as if he's looking for someone.

He's got the kind of hair that I love. Just enough to grab onto, but short enough to still be considered clean cut. His strong jaw sets in a grimace, like he's tense about what he just read on his phone. It's ironic that one person can find joy by texting the deceased, while here another clearly has only found misery from communing with the living. Maybe I'm not doing so bad after all.

When his gaze connects with mine, he gives me a polite half-smile that has the cutest dimple I have ever seen. He's the kind of man I'd make a sandwich for.

Finishing up my coffee, I take that as my cue to leave, reminding myself that even if the man with the cutest dimple I've ever seen was gay, there is absolutely no way I'm ready to date again. Right? Although, it's been far too long since I've had sex, and I've spent far too much time with my hand lately, my heart is only so big, and there's only room for one person: James.

LIAM

CHAPTER 7

My gaze is jumping all over this coffee shop in a frenzy. I obviously look like an idiot since the guy across from me is staring. I conspicuously glance back down at my phone. The unknown number that has been texting me this past week is in this very coffee shop. *Right now*. What are the odds of that?

To top everything else off, these messages have turned into something else entirely. From today's context I'm beginning to understand that this isn't an ex-boyfriend situation. It's a person-is-dead situation, and quite frankly, I have no idea how to handle this. There is nothing worse in the world than grief. I've seen that firsthand.

The mere fact that this woman is texting her dead lover has hit me like a brick on the head. My new phone number is his old number. I've got to fix this mix up now before it gets any worse than it already is.

Shit. What do I even say to her?

Looking around the coffee shop again, I notice a handful of women who are sitting alone. They're each busy on their phones or computers, typing away. One woman has her earbuds in talking and typing at the same time, obviously in a business meeting, so it's not her. If I text her back now, I can try to see who this person is, in the flesh. I quickly type out something, hoping she sees it before she has the chance to leave.

Hey. I'm sorry I haven't texted you back sooner, but you've been texting my new number. I thought it was just a random wrong number, so I didn't reply, assuming I'd not hear from you again, but I see now that you may think you're texting some- one you really miss. I'm very sorry for your loss, and I hope you can find some peace soon. PS—I agree with Nora. I love *The Breakfast Club*.

The minute I hit send, my ears perk up, listening for any type of text message notification. My eyes move around the coffee shop, seeing if anyone is picking up their phone.

What are the chances that we would be in the same place at the same time? *The Cup Connection* is just a short walk from my apartment. I just started coming here when I'm working from home after realizing how sad my apartment is to look at.

I keep looking around, but no one has picked up their phone. No noti- fications sound above the sound of coffee grinding and clinking glasses.

Damnit. I really wanted to see this girl who likes to watch cheesy movies in her underwear.

CHAPTER 8

On the short walk home, my phone dings. Figuring it's Nora demanding I pick up some type of food, I yank it out of my coat pocket. I'm not making any pit stops today. If she wants sushi, she can damn well get it herself. The name that pops up on my lock screen has me stopping in my tracks. Someone behind me slams into my back.

"*Ooophf!* Dude! What the—"

I quickly apologize to the woman I roadblocked and make my way to the nearest store front. Hiding under the awning, my hands shake as I hold up my phone.

James.

James texted me back?

No. This can't be right. That isn't possible.

Tears spring to my eyes at the sight of an incoming message under his name. They threaten to spill over in front of everyone walking down this sidewalk. I feel like I'm in some alternate universe where this could be possible. With shaking fingers, I open the message, blinking back the tears.

Holy. Fucking. Shit.

I've been texting a real live person this entire time. I shudder, reality seeping in over how embarrassing this is, how pathetic I must have sounded. This random person has been reading all my feelings for the past week and hasn't said a thing until now.

I power walk home so I can find Nora and let her have it. This was her stupid idea, so realistically, this is all her fault. She insisted I talk to James, and now this stranger knows all my deepest thoughts.

I'm going to kill her. The only positive here is that I didn't talk to James about how much I miss sex with him. I mean, there's that at least. Gotta look on the bright side.

"*Noraaa*!" I bellow as soon as I burst through the door.

Stomping into the living room, I find her sprawled out on the couch in her ugly pink bathrobe, watching some chick flick. Fishsticks is beached on the cushion next to her, belly up, fast asleep.

Nora scowls at me disapprovingly. "What? I'm at the part when they finally kiss, so whatever you have to say better be important."

"I've been...texting...James," I sputter, out of breath.

Shit. I really didn't want to have to admit that out loud.

Her jaw drops at my confession. "You've been...what?"

"Remember how you said to talk to James? Well, I've been talking to him! But...he's someone else!"

I'm completely aware that I'm not making any sense as soon as the words leave my mouth.

"*Whoa, whoa, whoa.* Back up. Back *waaay* the fuck up," she says, putting her hand up.

She's looking at me like I'm completely unbalanced. I guess this little admission is important enough for her to pause the movie because she grabs the remote and does just that.

I sit down on the side of the couch that isn't currently occupied by Fishsticks. I don't need a face full of scratches right now. I've been through enough trauma today.

"Okay. You said to talk to James, right? Well, I have been...but...on the phone. Like texting, I mean. And it turns out that someone else has his phone number now!"

Nora shakes her head as if I'm the stupidest person on the planet. "Well, I mean, that makes sense. Didn't you know they recycle phone numbers?"

I stare at her in utter disbelief. "Well, yeah! But I didn't think of that! Clearly!"

I really, really, really did not think about that. I've been texting a *recycled person.*

"So, this *someone*… What? They texted you back and said you've got the wrong number? So what? Why are your panties all in a twist?"

"It's embarrassing, Nora! Embarrassing! I said…*things*." Just thinking about what I shared makes me shudder.

She is totally downplaying this entire situation and acting like I'm overreacting. I'm not. This is serious.

"*Things*? Oh, my word. No way!" She snickers. "I told you to talk to James, *emotionally*, and you fucking sexted him? Here I thought you were grieving, but your shit mood is because you're a horny man beast!" Nora throws her head back in a fit of laughter. "This is magnificent, Jules. Magnificent," she says, slapping her leg, continuing to cackle. "Why didn't you tell me you wanted to get laid? I could have got you a profile on *The Tinder*." Covering the aggravating peals of laughter coming out of her green-smoothie-drinking-hole, she catches her breath and pats my leg. "No, seriously though. I'm happy for you, really. You're finally moving on. James would want that."

"NO! I didn't *sext*! You pervert!" I yell, smacking her arm away.

She stops laughing and eyeballs me. "Um, okaaay. What's the problem then? Just text back that you made a mistake. You're acting like this is the end of the world. Why were you texting him to talk to him anyway? I meant talk to him, like in your head, you idiot." She shakes her head at me, grabbing the remote off the arm rest to restart her movie.

What is she doing? This ass-chewing is far from over!

Slapping it out of her hands, I shout, "This is really your fault you know! You said—"

"Oh, my God! You're totally overreacting right now, Jules. Why are you…wait a minute! Is it a man? Is he gay?" Studying me as my face heats, her eyes widen. "Oh, my God! It is! That's why you're embarrassed! This is so cute. It's like a rom-com movie!" she squeals, getting off the couch to jump up and down.

I glance over at Fishsticks, who is now awake and looks perturbed that his nap has been interrupted. It's only a matter of seconds before he chooses a victim to punish, and it won't be me. I've had it. I walk down the hall, heading for my room.

"You are the worst friend! Like ever!" I yell, slamming the door behind me.

For you know, *dramatic* effect.

I take a long look around our room. Well, it's just my room now, not *ours.* Saying things like that is an almost impossible habit to break. I stare at James' dresser that takes up the entire wall next to the bed. It's time to go through his stuff. His dresser has been untouched since the day he died.

Inspecting the drawers, I pull out a shirt and give it a long sniff, trying to detect a hint of the way he used to smell. It's time to make this leap. It's time to start moving on. It doesn't smell like him anymore. It's just a shirt, nothing more. Even his scent has left me. Fishsticks has his sock. What I wouldn't give if I had his cat-like senses to still detect James' scent. Lucky bastard.

Going into the kitchen, I grab the garbage bags from under the sink. Nora gives me a questioning look.

"None of your business," I warn, marching back to my room.

As I start slowly bagging up the clothes, I find the shirt he wore on our first date. It's a blue silk button down T-shirt. If he wore it now, he would look like he stepped straight out of the 90's. The blue made his hazel eyes sparkle, accentuating the specks of brown in them. His brown hair would always fall over his right eye, making him look boyish and younger than he really was. I can't believe he kept it all these years. He looked so good in this shirt that all I wanted to do was rip it off him, and by the end of the night, I did.

Breathing deep, I put it in the bag with the others. It's okay. I can do this. I'll take these over to the secondhand shop tomorrow. Maybe some-one else can make happy memories in them. Maybe the magic of our first date can live on that way. I mean, if 90's fashion ever comes back in style.

Walking over to my own closet, I find everything still stacked up hap-hazardly. There was never enough room for all our stuff in this bedroom. When Nora moved in, I shoved all my stuff in there, unable to move James' clothes, as if he were going to come back for them one day.

I fold my shirts one by one and put them in James' old dresser. He's not here to use it anymore. I have to keep telling myself to fight off the choking sensation that's telling me I'm disrespecting his space. It's silly. I know it is.

Sitting down on the bed, I decide to suck it up and apologize to the person I've been accidentally texting. As embarrassed as I am, they deserve a response after having listened to me mourn all week. I can't imagine how disturbing it would be to get such depressing messages out of the blue.

> **Oh my God. I am so sorry. I didn't think this number would be active. This is my husband's old phone number. He died last year. Who thought I would be a thirty-year-old who texts their husband's old phone number like a basket-case? I apologize that you were the unintended lucky recipient who got to experience me and my craziness. Sorry again.**
>
> **And I agree, *The Breakfast Club* is a classic. My roommate has moved onto *Overboard* right now. My TV is like a time machine.**

I figure making a joke is the way to go, lightening the mood about the fact that I'm a lunatic. Bubbles pop up on the screen.

Holy crap. This person is typing back. I pace back and forth in my room, waiting for them to finish.

> **Would that be Nora? The one who laughed about your mother wanting you to join *Tinder*?**

Oh. My. God.

I'd forgotten about the *Tinder* message I sent. I put my head in my hands and let out a laugh. Yeah, I'll admit it, that was kind of funny.

> **JULES: The one and only. You officially know too much about my roommate and my mother. I hope you're not a crazy stalker.**

God, what if this person really is a whack job? I mean, I've watched *Dateline!* I know all about the crazies out there! You can't even buy anything off those sale pages on social media without the risk of being brutally murdered!

Well, I'll even the score. My name is Liam. Now you know something about me.

Liam. Huh. So, *I am* texting a man. Well, now I know that if I'm brutally murdered anytime soon, it's a man named Liam. I'll be sure to tell Nora that. Ya know, just in case.

LIAM: I also go to *The Cup Connection*. It's right down the street from my apartment. Hope that makes you feel better.

Yeah, it kind of does actually. I start typing another apology. God, this is embarrassing.

I'm Jules, and sorry again for bothering you about my crazy roommate and my insane mother.

My phone immediately dings with another notification.

Your mother sounds like a riot and so does Nora.

JULES: Yeah, they're great...until you meet them. LOL.

LIAM: LOL. My mom is the same. She has her own special brand of crazy.

I toss my phone on the bed, knowing there's no more pleasantries to be said. That was unexpected. This Liam seems like a cool, understanding guy. Maybe I won't end up dead in a dumpster after all.

CHAPTER 9

It's been a week since I last heard from Jules. Not that I should expect to hear back, but the mystery text woman with the beautiful name is stuck in my head. I'm constantly wondering how she's doing. Ever since I let her know it was me behind the phone number and not her husband, I feel like I've ruined her connection to him. I'm worried she needs someone to talk to, that she may need someone in her life who can understand the pain that comes with losing her husband.

After my dad died, I remember what my mom went through. Even though she was still an active mother, her spark went out when she lost Dad. Her eyes were lifeless. It's a sad thing, losing your other half. After seeing my mom reel with the loss of my dad, it made me realize that someone you love can disappear in an instant. No warning. Just gone with the snap of your fingers.

THE RIGHT WRONG NUMBER

I realize now, that's probably why it's been so difficult for me to get close to anyone emotionally. If you get attached, you have to deal with the very real possibility of losing them.

One-night stands require no commitment, no potential for loss. Feeling Jules' pain over her text messages has transported me back to seeing my mother fall into a fast depression. No matter what I tried, I wasn't able to help my mother much. The memories foster a pull for me to try and help Jules, to be there, even if just by text message. Maybe this time, I won't fail.

That pull urges my feet toward *The Cup Connection*...again. I'm dressed casually in a worn pair of jeans and a T-shirt that clings comfortably to my biceps. I may have looked at myself in the mirror a couple of times before leaving the house this morning. Not a big deal. Just ensuring I'm presentable. At least, that's what I'm telling myself.

I'm not trying to find the mysterious Jules. My excuse—I need to get some work done, and this is the place to do it. If I happen to see Jules here, it'll be pure coincidence, nothing else.

Glancing around, I notice a lot of women here, but most have men or friends accompanying them. A woman who texts her dead husband's phone doesn't sound like a woman who has company. Would it be weird if I texted her again? Just to check-in? Not any weirder than when I replied the first time, I guess.

I twist my teacup, fiddling with the handle and taking in the serene feeling of *The Cup Connection*. Its cozy ambiance helps settle my nerves.

I'll do it. It's just a friendly text. It's fine. No big deal. I just want to see if she's here. She said they came every Sunday afternoon at eleven. Grabbing my phone out of my pocket, I decide on something simple.

LIAM: Hi. It's Liam. How was *Overboard*?

I hit *send* before I can change my mind. Snapping my head around, I try seeing if my mystery woman is here. I don't know why I need to find her, but I do. I just need to be sure she's okay. I stare at the screen, willing for the bubbles to pop up and her to text me back. A giddy sensation trickles through me when they appear.

JULES: Fantastic. Who doesn't love Goldie?

I chuckle at the response, even though it's nothing special. I'm just glad I got one.

> **LIAM:** Just making sure you're okay. My dad died when I was young, and I remember what my mom went through.

> **JULES:** I'm sorry to hear about your father. Thank you for checking on me. That's very thoughtful of you. Fortunately, James and I didn't have any kids who had to go through this with me. I don't know how I would have handled being a single parent to a grieving child. That must have been incredibly difficult for both you and your mother.

> **LIAM:** It was a long time ago, but yeah, it wasn't easy. I can't imagine what you're going through.

> **JULES:** It's been a year now. I shouldn't be texting my dead husband's phone, telling him I miss the way he smells. You'd think I'd be over that by now.

I can still remember my dad's smell. She's anything but crazy. Going out on a limb, I decide to tell her this intimate confession I've never told anyone before.

> **LIAM:** No, I still miss the way my dad smelled. He worked as a mechanic, so he always smelled like motor oil and grease. I still can't walk into a garage without being sent back in time.

> **JULES:** You're making me feel better, like I'm not a basket case with a scent fetish. So, thanks for that.

> **LIAM:** Not at all. You sound like a total normal-case, and who am I to judge if you have a scent fetish? I'm sure there are way weirder fetishes out there.

JULES: My mother and Nora certainly convince me that I'm normal.

I bark out a loud laugh, then look around to see if anyone noticed that I'm sitting by myself and guffawing like an idiot. I've got to give Jules credit. Even though she's grieving, she still has a sense of humor. That's something that took my mother years to get back. It took her years to get back to even a semblance of her laughing jovial self. I look back down at my phone, deciding what I should write next. I want to keep this conversation flowing. I like...talking to her.

LIAM: I'm at *The Cup Connection* right now. Sometimes I come here when I'm working from home. Maybe we'll run into each other one day.

Shit. Did I just drop a hint? What am I doing?
Fuck it. I think I would like to run into her someday.
Take the hint Jules. Please, take the hint.

JULES: Yeah, maybe.

LIAM: If I ever see someone wearing an 80's movie T-shirt, I'll assume it's you.

JULES: Nah, I was a 90's kid. Even though I can appreciate a good 80's movie. What about you? You rockin' the 50's era? Life begins after retirement and all that?

I bark out yet another laugh. Do I sound like I have an AARP card or is she just giving me crap? How does this woman make me laugh so much? I haven't laughed like this in God knows how long.

LIAM: Nope. I'd be rocking a 90's shirt too.

I scroll up, trying to find our earlier messages. I remember seeing that she was around my age. Well, now she knows I'm not an old man, coming here for a senior's discount on coffee.

It's ironic how I grappled with how to keep the conversation flowing because before I know it, two hours have gone by. My fingers hurt and

I've gone through two cups of coffee that I didn't even need. The work I had planned on doing has gone to the wayside. It'll get done another day. I'd much rather spend two hours talking to Jules. I can't remember the last time I've texted someone this much or for this long. And if I had, I don't remember it because it sure as hell wasn't this enjoyable or memorable. She's an absolute delight.

I know it was just a mix up, a wrong number, but maybe it's the right wrong number after all.

JULES

CHAPTER 10

After Nora's excruciating gym routine, she forces me to go down the street and wander the local farmer's market so she can get whatever vile produce she puts in her smoothies. I wander over to a stall that has fresh, local honey. James used to buy my mom this honey for her tea. I'm lacking in the son department, so I'll pick her up a jar to make amends, plus carrying on the tradition for him is comforting.

I peek over to find Nora and see her in the stall next to mine, eyeing up some old lady's cross-stitch wall hangings. For fuck's sake. She better not even think about it. I will not tolerate kitschy *Live, Love, Laugh* signs in our apartment.

"Hey, you want any of this celery for your smoothies?" I ask, trying to distract her from whatever she's thinking about buying.

"Yeah. Grab an eggplant, too! Your mother wants to make us eggplant parmesan for dinner next week," she yells from the stall next to me.

Shit. I forgot my mother was coming over for dinner. Good thing I have Nora around to remember this stuff for me.

Mom does make a mean eggplant parmesan though. If there's one thing that I love the most about my mom, it's her cooking.

I find a table that contains a large pile of eggplants and sigh. I don't know how to pick an eggplant. Is there some secret to it? How do you know if an eggplant is good or bad?

As I go to grab one to inspect it, another hand brushes against mine. I immediately snatch my hand back and glance over, seeing a man with a small smirk on his face. As the corner of his lip turns up, I realize I know this man. I know this dimple.

"Oh, oops...um...sorry. Wrong eggplant," I barely stammer out.

He smiles even wider, his dimple in full force now. Holy shit. I nervously shift my weight from side to side, realizing this is the guy from the coffee shop the other day. I could never forget that dimple. Or that sexy tattoo that takes up his whole arm. The pattern is mesmerizing, the shades of black intertwining together in an almost sensual way.

"You know how to pick out an eggplant? Because I'm clueless in the eggplant department," I squeak out.

"Not a clue. I'm new to this. My refrigerator is currently full of condiments," he says with a halfcocked smile.

He doesn't look like he needs eggplants in his life. He doesn't look unhealthy. The way that shirt clings to his muscular body tells me he must take care of himself.

He grabs an eggplant off the pile. "This is the one," he quips with a smirk. "I can feel it."

Damn. That smile could knock a man to his knees.

I pick up my own eggplant, moving it around in my hands nervously. "Alright, this one looks good to me," I say as I tuck it under my arm.

He pauses, staring at me for just a moment too long.

Oh God. Does he recognize me from when I gawked at him at the coffee shop? Shit.

I let out a nervous laugh. "Well, guess I'll go and get some celery. My roommate makes these vegetable smoothies...and yeah. They're disgusting."

"Celery just tastes like water with hair in it," he states, barking out a husky laugh.

An amazing laugh. I could get lost in that laugh. I want to hear it again. And again. And again.

"What did the father tomato say to the baby tomato while on a walk?" I blurt out.

What am I saying? I sound like I'm reading a joke from one of those popsicle sticks. He stares at me with that dreamy smile, and I stare at his lips for a moment too long.

"Um, what?" he queries.

"Ketchup!" I yell out way too loud.

He laughs again, and this time my body instantly responds. I have butterflies in the pit of my stomach. Freaking butterflies! I forgot those existed. It's been so long since I felt them flutter.

"Good one." He snickers.

"Alright. Well, um, I've got to go. My roommate is gonna end up buying cross-stitch wall hangings if I don't stop her."

"Yeah, can't have that," he jests.

I scurry up to the cashier with a handful of celery, honey, and one lone eggplant. He sidles up behind me, close enough that I can smell his musky cologne. I breathe deeply through my nose, defenseless to catch another whiff. It's earthy, like sandalwood with a hint of something sweet. He smells intoxicating, his scent filling the air around me with a sense of peace and calm.

Collecting my bag, I run my hands through my hair nervously, feeling the need to redeem myself for my juvenile popsicle stick joke. "Um, have fun with your eggplant!" I bark.

Sweet baby Jesus. *Have fun with his eggplant?*

What the hell is wrong with me? The more I talk the worse it gets! I can't seem to stop making a fool out of myself.

I dart out of the stall before he can respond to my verbal diarrhea and sprint toward the next booth. Looking around, I see so much *Live, Love, Laugh* shit that it makes me nauseous. This booth is an absolute atrocity. I don't see Nora, but my gut tells me by the hideousness of the products that she's in here somewhere.

"Pssst! Nora!" I whisper-yell, when I finally spot her perusing some tacky doilies.

Grabbing her by the arm, I haul her out of cross-stitch hell before she buys something awful to further pollute my home with her eclectic taste. Wielding around, she scowls at me, looking for an explanation.

"I saw a man and got an eggplant," I rush out.

"Okaaay? *And?*" she asks, lifting a brow.

"And...and he was cute. He grabbed the same eggplant as me. I saw him at the coffee shop last week too! Wait? Am I being stalked? I saw an episode on *20/20* that was just like this!"

Shaking her head at me, her expression is less than impressed by my predicament. "It's an eggplant Jules, c'mon. Wait. Did you just say, *he was cute?* Like you checked him out?" she adds, her eyes the size of saucers.

Oh, for fuck's sake. She's tapping the toes of one of her red *Converse* shoes in her giddiness. Of course she'd make this a big deal.

"Well, how could I not! He was next to me, smelling like sandalwood, and touching the same eggplant as me! Then I made a joke about tomatoes," I confess, pinching my eyes shut to blot out the humiliating memory.

"A joke about tomatoes?" she asks, looking at me like I've grown two heads.

"Yeah, about ketchup. It was horrible. Oh, shit. I think I may have lost my ability to flirt!"

The realization hits me like a ton of bricks. How am I ever going to have sex again if I make tomato jokes when I find a person the least bit attractive? I mean, I can't be celibate for the rest of my life. I've been out of the game way too long. I have only been with James for the past ten years. I'm only thirty-six. What if I live to be seventy-five? That'd be thirty-nine years without sex. My dick could fall off!

"Oh, my God. You have a crush on *Tomato Guy*!" Nora exclaims, jumping up and down.

"I do *not* have a crush on Tomato Guy!" I angry whisper, but then another realization hits me. "Oh, no. I just flirted with someone over eggplants, and...James. What about James?" I gasp, covering my mouth.

No. I just *badly* flirted with someone...and didn't think about James, not even once.

Nora flings her arms around me and hugs me. "You checked someone out, Jules! It doesn't matter if it worked or not. The point is that you *tried* to flirt! I'm so proud of you!"

Why is she acting like I got a job promotion? I just told a lame joke about tomatoes and simultaneously dishonored the memory of my dead husband.

Shoving her off me, I growl, "No, I don't flirt. I can't! *James*! Did you forget about James? Oh, God." The reminder that I in fact did, has tears springing to my eyes.

"Jules, you can't go your whole life and not ever flirt with someone again," she soothes, holding onto my shoulders and looking me straight in the face. "That's neither healthy nor plausible. You didn't commit a crime. Okay?"

"Whatever. Can we just go home now?" I croak out.

I don't know how to feel about any of this. My body says this is a pivotal moment, it reminds me I'm still alive, but my mind is displaying a huge stop sign with flashing lights like a warning signal. These past few days have been a whirlwind.

A week ago, I was lying in bed refusing to move, and now I'm texting a stranger and flirting at the farmer's market. I miss James with every ounce of my being, but this past week things have been...well...*better.* I've been making connections with humans again. And shit, the thought of having sex with someone besides my hand again? Even though there's a cloud of guilt, it still feels like a step in the right direction.

Maybe I just need to bury myself in my mattress and sort it all out. I've been safe on my mattress for the last year. Everything will be fine once I get there.

"Wait! Look at that! Over there!" Nora yells, running into a booth across from us that has a toilet paper holder that looks like a cow.

I just flirted about tomatoes, got turned on over my hand touching the same eggplant as a dimply stranger, and she's atrocity shopping? Stomping off in the other direction, I almost wish she could hear me muttering that our friendship is now dead to me. I am not a shit friend, but I'm going home. No way am I commemorating my bull in a china shop behavior this afternoon with a toilet paper holder that looks like a cow.

JULES

CHAPTER 11

"I hate laundry day," I sigh, glancing in Nora's direction.

She's folding her T-shirts with her clothes-folding board, making sure every crease is perfect. Who has that much zeal over laundry?

"Well, I'm just glad you're finally participating in household chores again. I was tired of washing your dirty underwear."

"I never asked you to wash my clothes!" I retort.

I could very well have washed my own clothes, but Nora is strict on laundry day. It's not my fault that I sometimes slept through Sunday morning wash sessions. I was a grieving man, damnit. I didn't have the time or energy to wash my entire ass or my clothes.

"Yeah, well, if I didn't, your mother would be over here more than she already is. I love her to death, but there's only so much I can take."

"Well, look at me now. Adulting and shit!" I reply, tossing my shirts in the laundry basket without folding them. I can practically hear her brain grumbling about what a heathen I am for not folding my clothes properly.

"Calm down. I made space in the closet. I'm going to hang them up," I mutter before she can protest my lack of folding skills.

"Yeah, I noticed James' clothes bagged up by the door the other day," she ventures, her mouth turning into a slight frown.

"Baby steps," I declare.

I may be the tortoise and not the hare, but as they say, slow and steady wins the race. Fuck that hare anyway. I'm not a leaps and bounds kind of guy, unless it's a lame ass impromptu joke to a stranger about vegetables.

"You're like an actual human again! I'm so proud I got you here!" Nora beams, looking at me with smug satisfaction in her eyes.

"I'm not letting you have all the credit. It wasn't just you."

I won't deny that Nora has been a huge help to me. She's always been right by my side, but sometimes you need to get an outsider's perspective, and Liam happened to be the one to give it to me. I may have never met him, but he's helped me over the past week almost as much as Nora's nagging has over the past few months.

"What do you mean it wasn't just me? I didn't see anyone else stuffing your dirty clothes in the washing machine."

"I've been…texting that *Recycled Person*."

"*Recy*...wait. You're still texting the person that has James' old phone number?"

"Actually, yes. He makes me feel...*less crazy.*"

When Liam told me that he still misses his dad's smell, I almost cried happy tears. I'm not insane. It is completely normal to sniff the pillows and clothes of a dead person.

"*Less* crazy? You've been texting a random person like he's your therapist?"

"No! It's not like that! I can't explain it, but he makes me feel, well, normal."

"Are you and him, like, seeing each other? Are you sexting too?" she asks, her eyebrows shooting up to her hairline.

"What the hell! What is your deal with sexting? No!"

"Hey! I'm all for *sexty times*. Nothing wrong with it. I think you could use it," she says with a laugh.

"It would still involve my hand," I grumble.

My hand has had a serious workout this past year. I'm surprised my right hand isn't more toned than my left. Maybe I should look into getting a sex sleeve thing or whatever they're called. Add a little variety to my solo sexy times. Hm.

"Yeah, well, at least sexting would make the experience much more exciting."

"I don't want to talk about this with you."

I can only imagine that what Nora calls *Sexty Time* might actually be much more exciting than all the solo time I've been having lately now that my body is remembering it has needs. At least I could hear some dirty talk that isn't porn. Or read it off a text. Whatever.

"How long has this been going on for?"

"A few weeks."

"Holy shit, Jules! *A few weeks?* I'm super proud of you. You're going to the gym, doing household chores, and now I find out you're conversing with humans who aren't me or your mother. Hell yeah!" she says, putting her hand in the air for a high five that I refuse to return.

"Okay, enough. I get it. I was a miserable human being for a year. No need to rub it in my face."

I've learned that grief is such a fucked-up thing. You feel guilty for trying to move on from a person, but you also feel guilty for being miserable to everyone around you. I think I'm at the turning point now though, because at least I've realized that I was a miserable bastard. There is no way I would have even considered that a month ago. I want to be better. I want to do better.

"I'm not," Nora defends. "I really am proud of you. I mean it."

"Yeah, thanks. Wanna watch a movie tonight?" I ask, trying to change the subject.

"You...want to watch a movie...with me?" she asks, watching me while I fold my old *Nirvana* T-shirt hastily.

It's a 90's era T-shirt, that's for sure. I've had it since college, and the logo is faded but still readable. Maybe I'll wear this one next time I go into *The Cup Connection*. If Liam were there, I wonder if he would recognize me because of it?

"Liam and I talk about movies. He likes the same stuff that you do. It's gotten me in the mood," I say with a shrug.

"*Liam*? That's the *Recycled Person*?"

"Yep, he does have a name you know, so you can stop with the little air quotes now."

"Well, if he's got you down for a movie night, I like him already!" she says, jumping up and down excitedly.

There was a time I couldn't even fathom having a movie night without James. James and I always had movie nights with Nora when we could. If Nora wasn't around, we made sure to have movie night pantsless. Not having James here for the tradition seemed wrong. It was like I was saying I was comfortable doing all the things without him that I used to do with him, and I couldn't bear the thought of that. There were so many times I stopped myself from moving on out of loyalty, so many times I wouldn't let myself feel any sort of happiness. I thought that being happy meant that James didn't matter anymore.

None of that is true. Yes, James is gone, but I can't let myself be miserable for the rest of my life. I know he wouldn't want that for me. It's time to let myself be happy for me and everyone around me too.

CHAPTER 12

Plopping down on my uncomfortable leather couch, I bounce on the stiff cushion and flip on the TV. There's not even an imprint of my ass on this thing, showing how little I actually relax. My face is usually buried in my laptop, reading lines of never-ending code until my head throbs. I've made this weekend a work-free weekend, but the only thing it made me realize is how lonely I am. I fill my time with work to mask it, to make myself believe I'm not lonely and that I'm just busy. I have no one to share little moments with so I make sure I don't make time for sad, solitary moments by filling up my time with work. My father is dead, my mother lives across the country, and Oscar? Well, I need a longer break from him than I realized.

I flip mindlessly through the movie list on Netflix. Tommy Boy pops up, and I let out a chuckle, immediately reminded of Jules, the Jules who exists only in my phone. I want to change that. I want her to exist in real life, not some fake phone life.

I feel this pull, like the universe somehow destined us to meet. I know it's crazy and outlandish, and it's the stuff of the movies, but does Jules feel the same way I do about this random coincidence? I know that's what this whole situation really is—a random ass coincidence. A wrong number. But over the last few weeks, I've grown to love our quirky conversations and look forward to seeing her name pop up on my phone. Now, even watching TV has me thinking about her.

I pick my phone up off the coffee table, debating. Fuck it. I'm going for it. I'm just going to ask her to meet me. As friends. I glance up at my TV, searching for a conversation starter.

Does Nora like *Tommy Boy?*

I set the phone on the table in front of me like distancing it from myself will take away the rush of anxiety about what I want to ask, however, it immediately vibrates with a response. Grinning, I wonder if she was waiting for me to text her.

JULES: Everyone likes *Tommy Boy*...

Ha. She's totally right. I love *Tommy Boy.*

LIAM: I'm bored and watching it on *Netflix*. It made me think about you and Nora's movie obsession.

Telling her I thought about her...was that too much? Shit. No taking it back now.

JULES: Guess Nora and I are watching *Tommy Boy* tonight then.

Oh, really? Interesting. Sounds like someone doesn't mind that I was thinking about her. Here goes nothing.

ME: I've been thinking that maybe we could meet up sometime. No pressure. Just...we seem to en-

joy talking via text, and I thought we could do that in person?

There. I said it. Sort of. I rambled, sure, but I put it out there.

Leaning back onto the couch, I wait for her response. If she says *no*, she says no. No big deal.

Who am I kidding? I'm hoping those little bouncing dots are about to bring me an affirmative reply.

JULES: We could. It would be nice to talk to some-one besides Nora. I've been pretty shut in this past year, but I'm really trying to get out more.

ME: I'm glad you're trying. That's what matters. What are you up to now?

It's Saturday, the weekend. Maybe we could meet for an afternoon lunch today. Shit, I'm probably jumping the gun, but now that I've put it out there, I want for it to happen, like yesterday.

JULES: Lying in bed, mentally preparing myself for dinner with Nora and my mom.

ME: What are you wearing?

Fuck. That was meant to be small talk so I could picture what she'd look like walking into a restaurant. Why does it sound so dirty?

Damnit. Can I un-send a message on this thing? Fumbling my phone, I quickly type, anything to save my ass.

LIAM: Sorry. I meant "to dinner". What are you wearing to dinner?

Crap. She probably thinks I'm a creep, judging by the lack of reply. How do I get my foot out of my mouth?

LIAM: I realize that sounds like too much. I just... was trying to get an idea of you. Visualize who I'm talking to. Is that weird?

Over the past few weeks, we've chatted enough that I've garnered little bits of information. She has wavy brown hair. I'm guessing she's thin judging by how she's said her mom and Nora are on her ass to gain some weight. She works out several times a week, so she must be in some sort of decent physical shape.

They're all tiny puzzle pieces that I've been trying to put together to create a picture of this person whom I've rapidly grown a kinship with under the most unusual circumstances. Yet, it's not enough. I…want more.

I don't want just an *idea* of her. I want to know the real her, every living color, but now I probably just blew the odds of that happening with my eagerness. That's the thing about Jules though. She makes me drop my filter. I've never felt more free, truer to myself than when I'm chatting with her. There are no smoke screens, no expectations.

JULES: No need to apologize. I'm laughing at your "too much" comment because I'm in my underwear at the moment.

Wow. Okay. I wasn't expecting that.

The idea of her that I've longed to learn turns into something entirely different now that she's planted that visual in my head. She's on her bed…in her underwear?

Jules is on her bed in *only* her underwear while texting *me*. My concerns over "too much" have just flown out the window. Is she…flirting with me? Only one way to find out.

LIAM: Sexy. What color?

JULES: Black. What are you wearing?

A smile splits my face, knowing she's wondering about me too. I'm not sure how we got here, but my cock is starting to strain through my jeans. It's crazy, absolutely fucking crazy it's jumping to attention for someone I've never met, but at the same time it feels right, like I've connected with her more than any other woman in my life. The fantasy of her svelte skin on her stomach meeting the waistline of black panties has me salivating. My fun-loving, movie-quoting Jules, sprawled out on her bed, texting *me*. She could be doing anything right now, but she's texting me, asking me what I'm wearing.

Fuck.

Yanking my belt buckle free, I kick my pants to the floor. I was going to hop in the shower…later. Like…a few hours from now, but she doesn't need to know that.

> **LIAM: I'm actually taking off my jeans right now.**

> **JULES: Ah, so we match. Lol. Okay. Fair is fair. What color is your underwear?**

> **LIAM: Blue. Well, they were. I just took them off.**

Typing bubbles appear and then disappear several times. I don't think I've ever held my breath this long. Did I just ruin the best *almost-friend-ship* I've never had?

> **JULES: Um…you went there. Lol. Okay. You're out of clothes. Now what?**

That sounds like a challenge. Maybe I just want it to be a challenge, but the rise and fall of my chest have caution thrown to the wind. I know exactly *what now*. It's the same thing I always crave from Jules—to know more. Today though, I want to know more about things we've never discussed. I *am* out of clothes, but I'm far from out of ideas.

> **LIAM: Tell me what you like.**

There's a brief silence, but the typing bubbles finally appear. Once they start bouncing, her message comes through as though there was no hesitation once she decided on her response. That a girl.

> **JULES: I like to be kissed….**

Heat blooms in my abdomen at the admission. That was brave of her, and I'm thankful as fuck for it.

LIAM: Where? Your mouth? Your throat? Your nipples? Tell me.

JULES: Yes. All those places.

LIAM: Where else?

JULES: Down my stomach. Up my thighs.

I fist my cock at the honesty. I'm already rock hard, my tip glistening. I give my shaft a long gentle tug.

Fuck. When has texting ever been such a turn on?

LIAM: I wish I could touch you right now.

JULES: What would you do if you could?

LIAM: I'd kiss my way up your neck. Nip your earlobe. Make you feel so good, you'd be shaking.

JULES: Are you touching yourself?

Easiest answer I've ever given:

Yes.

Chest heaving, I rub my thumb through the precum on my tip, using it to slicken my length. Stroking faster, my hand becomes nothing but a filthy-sounding blur.

JULES: Me too. Are you close?

Oh, fuck yes. This woman, doing this for me, with me. Open and bold.

LIAM: Yes. So close. Just by thinking of you in your underwear.

JULES: Are you gonna come for me, Liam?

My name. God, I wish I could hear her say my name.

LIAM: Yes. I'm close. What would you do to me?

JULES: Lick you. Lick you everywhere. I'd use my tongue all over your body, licking up all your juices. Swallow you right down.

LIAM: Fuuuck.

JULES: I would come so hard for you. I want to come so hard for you right now.

LIAM: Do you like it hard?

JULES: Right now, I'd want it hard.

Thank God she's on the same page as me because I can't stop. We've entered fantasy land, so I give her the script of my fantasy unabashedly, telling her things I've never said in person to another partner.

LIAM: Fuck yes. Imagine me slamming you against your headboard, fucking you from behind.

JULES: Would you smack my ass too?

LIAM: Yes. Hard. And demand that you come for me.

JULES: Fuck yes. Tell me more.

LIAM: You like that? You like it rough?

JULES: I'd have you hold me down while you make me tell you who I belong to. I'd want you to growl 'mine' in my ear until you came everywhere.

LIAM: Holy shit. Jules….

Where the fuck has this woman been my entire life? I've never been so grateful for a mis-text. I never knew I'd want to growl that anyone was mine, but I think she just found my kryptonite. My balls are ready to burst at the idea.

LIAM: Fuck yes. Mine. You'd be mine. Shit. I need to come. Make me come. Tell me to come.

JULES: Come for me, Liam. Would you moan my name? Telling me how good I'm making you feel while I scream your name?

As the images fill my head, my hand moves wildly. Hips rocking into my grip, I come with a long shudder. Hot thick ropes launch up onto my stomach and chest. My head falls back on the couch with a grunt, totally spent.

Holy Shit. I've never done that before. What's the protocol for sexting? I pick up my phone off the cushion next to me where I dropped it, quickly typing out a text so I don't leave her hanging.

LIAM: Did you come for me, Jules?

A loud, long buzz pulls me out of my post orgasm haze. Who the hell is buzzing my apartment? Using my underwear, I give my cum-covered stomach a quick once over and then yank on my jeans. I walk to the intercom in long strides while buttoning my pants.

Pressing the button, I bark into the intercom, "Yeah?"

"Let me up!" Oscar's voice demands.

Son of a bitch. Not now. I buzz him in. Two minutes later he barges through the door. Not even a knock. Typical.

"Dude, have you ever heard of calling!" I snap.

Oscar always does this. It makes me wonder if he was raised in the wild. He is the most mannerless person I've ever encountered. It used to be amusing, but it's lost its appeal.

He looks me up and down, brow arched. "What were you doing? Why aren't you wearing a shirt?"

"Nothing!"

My tumultuous pitch makes it obvious that I was up to something, but I'm not telling him a damn thing. He already knows way too much about my life, up my ass every free minute of the day.

He glances around the apartment like he's looking for someone. "Are you...with someone?" he asks, glaring at me accusingly.

"No. No one's here. What do you want?" I bark, marching over to the couch and picking up my phone.

I smile when I see a text from Jules.

I came so hard for you.

My face heats up. I can feel the blush running down my neck. She came for me, and for some reason I can't explain, I'm ecstatic about it.

"Dude, what's that?" Oscar asks, stomping over to me.

"What's what?"

"That smile. That dreamy ass smile on your face. Who are you talking to?" He looks at my phone. "Are you talking to that I-miss-you-girl?"

"None of your damn business."

Eyes roving over my chest, he seems to connect the dots of why I could possibly be half-naked.

"Were you...*sexting* her?" he says, chuckling under his breath.

I don't answer quickly enough. His eyes widen, his mouth going agape.

"Holy shit. You so were! *Tell. Me. Everything*," he demands, accentuating each word with a poke to my chest.

"Why are you here?" I ask, trying to change the subject.

He walks over to the refrigerator with an amused grin, ogling the eggplant on my counter. "What's with all this produce, dude? And where's the beer?"

I shove the refrigerator door closed with my hip. "There's no beer."

He glances around my apartment suspiciously. "What's going on with you, man? No beer, all this fruit, and not giving me all the sordid details of your *sextscapade*?"

"Just trying to eat better. Can't a guy eat a banana without getting the third degree?"

Oscar puts his hands up defensively. "Alright, alright. I was just stopping by, seeing if you wanted to catch the game at the bar." Glancing at my TV, he grimaces in disgust at *Tommy Boy*, adding, "But I can see

THE RIGHT WRONG NUMBER

that you're obviously way more invested in this stupid 90's movie and sexting than football, so I'll see myself out..."

He looks at me quizzically like he's hoping I'll take him up on his offer. I won't.

For the love of God, can he just leave already? I have someone that just *came for me*, and I would very much like to respond.

"Nah, I've got to get some work done."

Shaking his head, the set of his mouth makes his disappointment evident. "Fine, but you're going to tell me about this new chick tomorrow at work."

"Fuck, fine," I respond, showing him to the door.

As he walks out, he gives a quick glance over his shoulder. "See ya tomorrow, bro."

"Yeah." I grunt, slamming the door shut.

Marching over to the coffee table, I pick up my phone. No new messages.

Great. I left her hanging too long. Did she have time to think about what we just did, and it scared her off? Stupid Oscar.

The panic has me feeling desperate. I don't even stop to second-guess myself, typing out a reply.

Meet at the coffee shop, next Saturday, noon?

JULES

CHAPTER 13

Holy. Shit. What the hell was *that*?

I just sexted a stranger, and it felt...well, it felt...okay. Actually, it felt epically phenomenal.

I've been worried about moving on from James. What would it be like to be with someone else? Would I feel like I was cheating on him? All these questions have been circling through my brain. I know Nora and my mom think it's time to start moving on, but it's easier said than done when your heart is still tied to someone else's. When your heart still beats for them and theirs no longer beats at all, you're left holding all the feelings, and there's nowhere to put them. But this? Tonight?

Baby steps, I guess. Very good baby steps. I have to start somewhere.

Leaning forward, I grab a few tissues off the nightstand and clean myself up. I have thirty minutes until my mother arrives. I need to talk to Nora before Mom gets here.

Liam wants to meet. Like in *real life meet*. The thought flickers a spark of excitement in me that's overruled by the idea scaring the fuck out of me in every way possible. If we meet, it becomes real. If we meet, I have to actually go through the motions of going there, talking to him in person, and…moving on from James. I absolutely need Nora's support for this. Hell, I always need Nora's support.

Staggering down the hall on my post-orgasm legs, I find Nora in the kitchen slicing an eggplant. She's shaking her hips to a headache inducing pop song and using the knife as a microphone.

"Hey, can we talk for a second? Um, preferably while you're not wielding a knife?" I ask, gesturing to the large blade in her hand.

Nora sets the knife down apprehensively. "Okay, but first, we need to talk about Fishsticks. I think we should take him to the vet," she says with a worried tone to her voice.

Glancing over at Fishsticks where he's lounging on the arm of the couch, I catch him glaring at us. He has James' sock tucked underneath his obese body. By the daggers he's throwing at me, he clearly knows what we're talking about. Just one more reason why that damn cat gives me the creeps.

"Don't say *that word* out loud. He *knows*," I whisper.

"He needs to go to the v-e-t. All he does is eat, and I've been having to fill up his water dish like three times a day," she says.

Glancing at Fishsticks, she scolds, "Don't you look at me like that. It's for your own good!"

"He drinks so much because he's lugging around twenty-five pounds! His belly practically touches the floor!" I exclaim, pointing to the massive beast.

Nora scowls at me, letting me know that I won't win this argument. Sighing, I roll my eyes.

"Okay, fine. The v-e-t James used is saved in my phone. I'll make him an appointment, but you're coming with me. The last time we had to stuff his ass into a c-r-a-t-e, I looked like I went through a woodchipper," I moan, remembering the event all too clearly.

I don't want to relive that experience again, but I have no choice. Fishsticks is way overdue for his annual checkup. Again, here I am, being a bad cat dad and not taking care of my responsibilities because I was too caught up in my own grief to see what was going on around me.

Nora's posture relaxes, and she shrugs, soaking in her victory. "Okay, that's settled. Now what did you want to talk about?"

70

"Oh, um. Well...I was wondering if you could do me like...a favor?"

"Probably not, but feel free to ask," she chuckles, waving her hand at me dismissively.

"I kind of have a well...a date. Maybe? Not a date. A meet-up kind of thing?" Scrubbing my hands over my face, I groan, "I don't know what it is actually."

What *is* this thing? It's not a date. It's just two people meeting who got thrown together by pure coincidence. Yeah, that's what this is. *Not a date. A coincidate.*

There. Yes. We're having a *coincidate.* Maybe all isn't lost in regard to my writing. Not if I keep coming up with winners like that.

While I've been trying to come up with what this meeting is, I swear Nora's mouth has almost hit the floor. "*A date?*" she shrieks.

"No. No," I caution, trying to correct myself before she gives me a hug so tight that my ribs bruise. "Remember how I was texting The Recyc...I mean...Liam? Well, he wants to meet up in person and get a coffee."

"Okay, but why are you asking me to go?" Her face scrunches in confusion and she returns to her dicing.

Why is she being so cavalier about this? Just a few weeks ago, she practically physically attacked me about Tomato Guy at the farmer's market.

"Because I watch *Dateline*! I don't want to end up in a dumpster. And maybe I could use, I don't know, *moral support.*"

"You really need to stop watching those true crime shows," she says, shaking her head. When she finally notices that I'm still standing here, looking as pathetic as I feel for being a coward, she sighs. "Okay, fine. When are we going on this thing that is *not a date?*"

"At noon on Saturday at *The Cup Connection.* Can you manage that?" I ask, putting my hands together, pleading.

"Only if you promise to make Fishsticks his v-e-t appointment. Tomorrow. I'm putting it on a *Post-It Note* after this, therefore it cannot be retracted."

Which means it's serious. Nora takes her *Post-It Notes* very seriously.

"Deal, but you have no idea what a disaster that's going to be," I warn, walking back to my room.

She's in for quite the surprise if she thinks Fishsticks is going to get into a crate willingly. Big battles are in our future.

I grab my phone off the bed, quickly typing out a response before I lose my nerve.

I'll sit in the corner with the aloe plant on the table.

*****

Sitting down in the uncomfortable wooden chair at our small dining room table, I grab my fork, ready to dig into my eggplant parmesan when my mother starts serving me a plate of salad. Like a damn child.

"Mom! I can get my own salad!" I say, swatting her hand away in protest.

"What's new with you, dear? It's been a week since I've seen you! Anything exciting happen?" she asks, chuckling under her breath.

I glance over at Nora, not knowing what she's told my mom. Their relationship has become far too close since James died. This constant talking and texting between them has got to stop. It's like I live with a damn spy rather than my best friend. God forbid I keep anything a secret around here.

"Oh, I forgot!" I exclaim, derailing her inquisition as I push my chair back and reach inside the cabinet. "I picked you up some honey at the farmer's market."

I know what she's getting at, and yes, I'm trying to avoid it. Like the plague.

"Oh, that was sweet of you. You know how much I love it in my tea! Did anything...um...happen when you got my honey?" she queries, hiding a grin behind her hand.

Glancing over at Nora, I scowl. "Damnit. You told her about The Tomato Guy, didn't you?"

Nora shrugs, a smirk on her face. My epically humiliating flirting skills have officially been broadcasted. At least they don't know about my *sexty time* with Liam. I get to keep some of my dignity.

"Mom, please. This is embarrassing. I made a terrible joke about tomatoes. The end." I say, leaving out the part where I told him to have fun with his eggplant. Fuck my life. I still can't believe I actually said that. I'm a fucking writer.

"Okay, I'll leave you alone about it," she promises, grabbing my hand from across the table, a knowing look in her eyes. "But I was just so glad to hear that you're getting back out there. I'm tired of seeing you so sad."

I can see tears starting to pool in her eyes. Her tears make me cave every single time, and she knows it. Down comes my guard like a crumbling brick wall.

"I may actually have an, um..." I relent, the sight of her concern weighing me down with guilt over not having my shit together. "Um, well, it's a...kind of date? A meeting? A *coincidate*? I don't know what to call it," I sputter before I can stop myself.

I know how much my grief has worn her down. I want her to know that I'm okay, or I will be, eventually. It's a terrible feeling having your mother worry about you this much when you're a grown ass man.

She claps her hands, bouncing in her seat. Her tears are replaced by a glow of happiness in her eyes.

That's better. I want her to be happy. I'm tired of the worry she's been carrying around because of me.

"Oh! How exciting! Did you use *The Tinder* I told you about?" she asks excitedly.

"No! Good God, no!" I exclaim, looking over at Nora, who is way too quiet. "Save. Me," I whisper, kicking her under the table.

"Hey!" she yells and kicks me back. Hard.

"Ow!" I yell, rubbing my shin.

Ugh. That's gonna leave a mark.

"Would you two just quit!" my mom yells. She sounds like she did when Nora and I were in the third grade.

"Um, well, we're taking Fishsticks to the v-e-t next week too," she says, purposefully changing the subject.

Good save Nora. Good save.

Mom looks over at Fishsticks who is sprawled out across the whole counter, taking up almost every inch of space. Her brow furrows, and she shakes her head. "That cat needs more than a vet. He needs an intervention."

At the word *vet*, Fishsticks scrambles to his feet and jumps off the counter, knocking over a stack of cups on his way down. He has his dirty white sock hanging from his mouth like a cat that lives on the streets. Damn! I didn't know he could move that fast.

CHAPTER 14

You're not a serial killer, right?

I let out a chuckle, reading Jules' last message. Man, she makes me laugh. Not many people can do that. I type out a response I hope will impress her with my own wit.

If I was a serial killer, would I admit that I was a serial killer?

JULES: Touché.

LIAM: So, are you saying it'd be weird if I was dressed up like a clown when I meet you?

God, I hope she knows I'm joking.

JULES: Please don't. You'll give off John Wayne Gacy vibes.

She totally picked up where I was going with that. Should it be such a turn on that she gets my jokes?

LIAM: Well, they say Ted Bundy was a handsome, charming guy.

JULES: You're a man who knows his serial killers. I don't know whether to be impressed or run for my life.

LIAM: I may have watched a documentary or two. LOL.

JULES: A fellow true crime junkie? Can we be best friends? Just promise not to make a lampshade out of my skin.

ME: Ha! No skin lamp shades here, promise.

I put my phone down just as Oscar makes an appearance in my office.

"You skipped lunch? Are you avoiding me or just avoiding telling me about your new girl?" he asks.

Making myself look busy with the papers on my desk, I reply with a huff, "Actually, I was avoiding *Hooters*."

He takes a seat in the chair across from my desk, settling in. "So, are you going to meet her or what?"

He will never let this go. I really don't want to hear his thoughts on Jules. I haven't felt this good in a long time, and if anyone could ruin it for me, it would be Oscar.

Studying him as I grind my teeth, wishing I could get back to the texting he interrupted, I decide on what kind of bone I can throw him. I'll give him the barest amount of information to quell his curiosity.

"Yep, a coffee shop on Saturday," I respond, folding my hands under my chin like it's no big deal to me. "Now go back to work. I'm busy," I say, nodding my chin toward my office door.

"No can do. I'm here for a reason this time. Boss wants to see you. Something about some charity event we have to attend. It's mandatory, so good luck trying to get out of it this time," he says with a smug cackle.

Oscar knows how much I hate these things. They are the bane of my existence. Walking around a room all dressed up, shaking hands with people I'll never see again. I mean, I get it. It's for a good cause, but why do I have to be there? It's not like I'm personally stuffing the pockets of the fund with five thousand dollars.

"Fuck," I cuss, rolling my eyes and getting up out of my chair.

Walking down the hall, I'm already trying to prepare an excuse to get out of this. The last time the office participated in one of these, I had some lame fabricated excuse about my mom. Note to self, don't use Mom as an excuse this time.

Stopping at my boss' door, I run my fingers through my hair to make myself look halfway presentable. Taking a deep breath, I knock and then swing open the halfway closed door. "Hey. Oscar said you wanted to see me?" I ask warily.

"Liam! Just the man I wanted to talk to!" he says in his deep, husky voice.

He's twenty years my senior with a head full of gray hair. My mom taught me to respect my elders, so the reminder of our age difference is not helping me muster the courage to find another lie. He crosses his arms over his desk like he means business. Yep. I'm screwed. I am not getting out of this.

"Yeah? What's going on?" I ask apprehensively.

"We have a charity event in two months, and I'm making this one mandatory for you since you missed the last one. This one is special. It's an auction!" he exclaims, like I should be excited.

Why would I be excited about a bunch of people auctioning off their crap? I don't want their crap.

I lift my brow. "A charity auction? What, exactly, is being auctioned off? Antiques?"

"No," he chuckles, grinning like I'm a fool. One of his big hands slams down on the surface of his desk for emphasis as he proclaims, "Dates!"

"*Dates....*"

Oh, fuck. Of course, I would be stuck attending *this* one. They're literally going to auction off people?

"Yep! And I want you to bid on one woman with the company charity fund!" he says excitedly.

"A woman? But…what if I don't want to go on a date with her?"

My company cannot make me go on a date. That's got to classify as some kind of sexual harassment, right?

"I don't give a shit if you go on the date or not, but you're bidding. No more than one thousand dollars. I'm putting you in charge because you're the only one in the office who seems to always get out of these events."

Okay. I can accept that. All I'll have to do is wave one of those little paddles and throw the company's money away for them. I'll bid on a woman and tell her afterward that she got off easy by not having to go on a date with a stranger who buys his dates. Heck, she'll probably thank me for saving her from the awkwardness. I mean, it's likely the contestants are forced into this too. Freaking charity events. Can't they just set out a can for people to drop money into?

"You got it," I assure him. "I'll do the bidding."

"Great! I'll send all the details to your email as soon as I get them," he says, looking back at his computer, telling me the conversation is over.

Walking out of his office, however, I wonder if he put me in charge of the bidding because I make excuses about how to get out of horrible charity events, or if it's because he thinks I need a date. I'm not that pathetic. I can get a date without bidding for one for God's sake.

Pulling out my phone, I glance at the newest message that Jules has left me. It's a picture of a very angry cat. The message underneath reads, **If anyone is a serial killer, it's this guy**.

I agree. That is one pissed off cat.

JULES

CHAPTER 15

"Alright, Nora. Let's do this! Where is the beast?" I grumble, walking down the hallway, peering around corners.

This is going to be a fucking nightmare. I feel like I need to wear those chainmail outfits that people wear to those Renaissance Faires in order to get out of this unscathed.

"Don't you dare let him see that thing! Keep it in the hallway!" she yells, gesturing to the crate wildly.

Putting the crate down, I sneak into the living room in stealth mode. The last time James and I attempted to do this, it took an hour. I'm betting it'll take at least two and a trip to the emergency room this time.

"What's your plan of attack?" I ask.

"I stuck some catnip in his food this morning. I'm hoping he'll be so high that he won't notice our covert operation." Nora beams.

"Fat chance. The amount of catnip it takes to make that cat high is obscene," I mutter.

Fishsticks is fast asleep on the couch, snoring, obviously coming down from his buzz. How much catnip did Nora scrounge up? Maybe this won't be as difficult as I thought. I start to sneak up on him, but the floor creaks beneath my feet. He jolts out of his catnip coma and onto all fours like he's ready to rumble.

I knew it. It was too good to be true.

"He doesn't look high," I say, throwing a stink eye at Nora. "In fact, he looks like his normal pissed off self."

Sneaking around to his other side, Nora whispers, "I'm hoping his responses slow down. Like he won't see what's coming until it's too late."

I kneel beside the couch and am greeted with a hiss. Holding my hand out in a feeble attempt to get into his good graces, I soothe, "Hey, Fishsticks. How was your nap, buddy?"

One of his beefy paws swats through the air with the speed of a cheetah. It's so fast, I don't have time to draw back. His sharp claws slice across the back of my hand.

"He got me!" I yank my hand back, staring at the three crimson lines across my flesh.

Just as I let out a yelp, Nora's hand darts under his belly like she's attempting to lift him up while he's distracted over his victory from maiming me. With amazingly *not-high* cat reflexes, he turns with a loud growl and lunges for her fingers, leaving a cat tooth imprint behind.

"Ow! Fuck you too, Fishsticks!" she screeches, tossing him back on the cushion and grabbing her finger.

Snatching the throw blanket off the couch as Fishsticks arches his back like he's gearing up for WWIII, I blurt, "I have an idea!" Tossing the blanket, I hold my breath as it balloons in a canopy over Fishsticks. His massive form shifts underneath it like he's searching for escape.

Fuck. We only have seconds.

"Grab him! Now!" I command.

Nora bomb dives on top of the blanket, hugging her arms around the Fishsticks-sized lump in the center of it. The throaty growl he emits is no less terrifying than if it weren't muffled by the thread count.

"Get the thing! Get the thing!" she yells at me, while wrestling with the huge lump under her arms.

"What *thing*?" I flail my arms, trying to figure out what she wants from me. Does she have a tranquilizer gun hidden somewhere as a back-up plan that she didn't tell me about?

"*The crate*, you idiot!" she grunts, clearly having to use all her strength to subdue James' precious, pissed off pet.

When I scramble back from the hallway with the crate, I hold it up to the edge of the couch cushion and swing open the door. Nora tries to put Fishsticks inside, but just as I told her this operation would end up, that goes to shit too.

"Why...is he...so fucking...fat?" she wheezes.

I don't know who's making more noise: her grunting or Fishsticks' unholy, livid sounds. Damn, he has gotten big. He wouldn't fit into a cat crate, so James and I bought a small dog crate instead, but now even that looks like it's shrunk. When Nora finally helps Fishsticks inside the dog crate, I slam the door shut just as he lashes out toward the opening. I really want to stick his special sock in there for comfort, but I don't dare open the door again for fear of retaliation.

Man, that only took like five minutes. Amazing! Blanket idea for the win! One point for Jules. Zero points for Fishsticks. Finally, I won at *something*.

"Awesome!" I exclaim as the latch clicks shut. "That was way easier than last time!"

Nora picks up the crate with a scowl. "Let's just get this over with," she huffs, attempting to carry the crate in one hand.

Fishsticks is so large and shuffling around in agitation that it sets the whole crate off balance, making it teeter back and forth in her grasp.

"Give him to me," I say, taking the crate from Nora. Her skinny arms clearly can't handle his weight. As soon as she hands him over, the strain of carrying him and the crate tugs my arm down like an anchor, making me shift to one side.

"Holy hell! He's gained way more weight than I thought!" I exclaim.

This crate must weigh at least thirty pounds with Fishsticks inside of it. I did not realize he had gotten this big.

Once Fishsticks is in the car, I almost have hope that this vet visit is going to be easier than I thought. It's only a fifteen-minute drive to the clinic, but the sounds that are coming from the back seat resemble those of a demon straight from hell. Nora turns up the radio trying to drown him out, but Fishsticks just mews louder.

The mix of Nora's dreadful pop music and Fishsticks possessed demon sounds is giving me a headache. As soon as we get in the parking lot, I jab the radio, turning off the music.

"I can't. I can't anymore. If there's a hell, I'm in it right now," I sigh, rubbing my temples.

Getting out of the car, I take the crate out of the backseat and bend over to peer at Fishsticks inside.

"There, there. Don't worry. Even though you hate me, I won't subject you to any more of Nora's singing," I soothe, patting the top of the crate like I'm saving a cat that actually loves me.

*****

There must have been a note in Fishsticks' file about his unsatisfactory behavior at the vet because the man who comes into our room doesn't look like a veterinarian. He looks like Hannibal Lecter. Dr. Theo's thick welding gloves go up his whole arm. Metal mesh gloves for this demonic cat, I can understand. Makes sense. I'll have to try that next time I have to wrangle Fishsticks, but the mask? Jesus. What happened the last time James brought Fishsticks' in that this guy is wearing a freaking welding mask?

"Oh my God, are you a *Mandalorian*?" I ask him. Glancing at Nora for confirmation, I add, "Is this real life?"

Dr. Theo backs away from the crate and lifts his mask revealing a grimace. "I remember what happened the last time Fishsticks was here. It wasn't pretty. This is…just a precaution. Now, let's try to take him out of the crate, but…slowly please," he adds just before lowering his mask.

Shit. It's bad when even the veterinarian is terrified of your cat.

As soon as I open the door, Fishsticks darts out and stumbles, looking up at me with pure disgust in his eyes.

"Oh, shit," I mutter, slowly inching toward the opposite corner of the room.

"Okay, Doc. He's not losing weight," Nora rushes out like she wants out of this room as badly as I do. "And I've had him on a diet for almost a year. All he wants to do is eat all day and all night. He also drinks so much water that I can barely keep the bowl filled before it's gone. Oh, and he needs his rabies shot updated, too.".

Nora and her whole water issue. My God, it's not rocket science.

"That's because he's obese, Nora. He's thirsty because even walking around the apartment is a complete work out for him," I argue, pointing at the snarling creature in front of us.

"Hm, well, I have a thought," Dr. Theo says, "but let's run some tests. In order to do that though, I'm going to have to sedate him. There's no way I can draw blood from him when he's acting like this." He points at Fishsticks accusingly whose tail is twitching agitatedly, and his fur is in a massive poof, making him look three times his size. I whip out my phone to take a picture of him in all his hostile glory. The next time Nora insists on taking him to the vet, I'm going to show her this and find a vet that makes house calls.

I'm also sending it to Liam. He thinks human skin lamp shades are bad? No serial killer is worse than this.

"Please do, be my guest!" I inform Dr. Theo.

I'm not even going to pretend that I wouldn't love to have a sedated Fishsticks. My fears of being a bad cat dad and having the ASPCA come after me are a distant memory now that I've seen an educated medical professional decked out in welding garb to examine my cat. A sedated Fishsticks sounds like a fantastic time.

"This will take a bit. Why don't you head out into the waiting room while my assistant and I try to calm him down," he says, sighing and gesturing for us to wait in the lobby.

As soon as Nora and I sit down in the empty waiting room, it sounds like a bomb goes off behind the exam room door. I can hear things clattering to the ground, yelling, and even a crash of what sounds like glass hitting the floor. I wince, glancing at Nora. Judging from the impressive height of her raised brows, she's hearing the severity of the commotion too.

Yeah, that's not good. I hope they don't make me pay for that. Sighing in unison, we sit back in the waiting room chairs.

After a few more minutes of listening to the soundtrack of Fishsticks giving the veterinary staff a run for their money, Nora flashes me a smirk and elbows me in the ribs. "Dr. Theo is kind of hot. You should ask him for his number."

"Really, Nora? Can you stop trying to set me up with people!"

I know she means well, but damn. I'm not her pet project. I'll find someone when I'm ready.

After a lot of magazine-flipping and disturbing noises, we're finally called back into the exam room. Fishsticks is on the table, not moving.

"Did you kill him?" I ask, hesitantly petting his belly in case he's just playing dead as a tactic to maim me.

"He's heavily sedated, and I mean *heavily*," Dr. Theo informs us, looking a bit worse for the wear and out of breath now that he's *dewelded* himself and I can see his disheveled hair. "He should sleep for the rest of the day."

"Are you sure he's alright?" Nora asks, looking the giant sleeping tabby over with wide eyes.

"Yes, but he has diabetes," Dr. Theo says bluntly.

"Diabetes? Cats can get diabetes?" I question.

I had no idea that was even a thing. Cats can get actual diabetes? Who knew?

"Yep, that's why he won't stop drinking water. Excessive thirst is one of the symptoms," he elaborates.

"Huh. Okay, so, uh, what do we do for that?" I ask nervously, twisting my hands together.

Oh my God, what if I kill James' cat? This can't be happening right now. I'll never forgive myself.

Dr. Theo sets down a batch of needles on the counter along with some pamphlets. "Insulin."

"You want us...to give Fishsticks...insulin? Via *a needle*? As in...*stick a needle* into his skin? You can't be serious," Nora deadpans.

She's right. He can't be freaking serious. That is just not possible.

"Yep, twice a day. Morning and night. I've written all the information down in his paperwork, and here is some in depth information about how the disease affects cats," he informs me, setting down so many pamphlets that it will take me all night to read them all.

"How are we supposed to give him a shot twice a day? He won't let us near him most of the time!" Nora snaps.

Dr. Theo shrugs. "You're going to have to figure it out. I can prescribe some sedatives, if need be, but I'd rather you both find a way to make this work first. Also, he needs to be on a special diet. You can purchase the food at the front counter. There are portion directions on the label. It's about fifty dollars a bag."

"Oh my God! This cat is going to run me out of house and home! And he doesn't even like me!" I yell.

Glancing up at the ceiling, I do what Nora suggested and talk to James. Babe, *you'd better be fucking happy.*

LIAM

CHAPTER 16

JULES: Still on for today at noon?

Hell yes, I'm still on for today. This meet-up we have planned is the only thing that got me through a chaotic work week filled with soul-sucking code and obnoxious inquiries from Oscar. Before I hop in the shower, I shoot Jules off a reply.

> **ME: What if the aloe plant table is taken? How will we find each other?**
>
> **ME: Btw, I know this sounds a little cheesy, but I'm really excited to finally meet you.**

Setting down the phone on the bathroom counter, I jump in the shower. I hear the notification go off while washing all the important parts.

I'm not planning on having sex since this is an afternoon thing, but still. Gotta make a good impression.

Slinging my towel around my waist, I walk to the bathroom mirror, swiping my hand over the fogged-up glass. Scrubbing my hand over my face, I decide to give myself a little trim. I like to keep my goatee neat and clean.

I flip over the phone and swipe the notification bar that says a picture message has come through. My heart skips a beat. A picture? Fuck yes. Finally, I get to find out what she looks like.

I click on the image, holding my breath and…

What. The. Fuck?

I step back from my phone, completely shocked by what's on the screen. My mouth gapes open and I'm pretty sure I'm making some type of gasping noise.

Holy. Fucking. Shit.

That…is a *man*. Not a woman. *A man.*

Jules, Jules, Jules. As in *Julie*? Or, fuck, I guess, *Julian*?

Oh my God.

I assumed *Jules* was short for *Julie or Julia*!

I assumed very fucking wrong.

Holy shit. This means that I…sexted a man.

I walk out of the bathroom in daze, still in my towel, and sink into the couch.

I told her…fuck! *Him*! I told *him* my name is Liam. Jules knows *I'm* a man. Right?

I swipe up on our conversation, re-reading, trying to find any hint that I missed that I was talking to a man and not a woman. Our sexts. Yes, that should tell me where the hell I missed this critical factoid. But… nope. Not even those give any indication that Jules has a dick.

Scrubbing my hand down my face, I let out a long sour chuckle. This is just my luck. The person I was getting to know, and beginning to really like is a man. This is just fucking great.

How can I have such a pang of loss in my chest over losing something that I never even had to begin with? Maybe it's the loss of the potential, the incredible sense of potential I thought this had to lead to something. It definitely felt like something special, a deeper connection than I've ever had with anyone I've known in the flesh. I mean, I really liked…I liked Jules for…*his* personality, not for whatever he looked like behind his phone. And if I'm honest, I guess I still do. He…he's a pretty cool guy.

But…the other feelings…now that I know he's a man? I've never…
Shit.

How the hell am I going to explain this to him? He could be on his way there already. I can't text a guy who lost his husband that I thought he was a woman the entire time we were talking and…sexting. He came out of his comfort zone for me. Shit. Bad choice of words. He also *came* for me. Fuck. He came for me. You don't get to be the first person someone moved on with and then end it with a text. Man or woman, that'd be way too callous.

Yeah. This conversation is the kind that needs to be done in person. Not how I imagined this Saturday panning out, but I have to go and explain this to him in person. I owe him that much. I can act like the grown ass mature man that I am. Just a huge misunderstanding. That's all. We can be friends. Buddies. Whatever.

Staring at my phone, the loss still weighs down my heart as I type out a message.

See you soon.

Shaking my head, I head back to the bathroom. I still need to make myself presentable. Grabbing my trimmers, I trim my slight beard, getting all the stray and unruly hairs. I'll wear something casual, a T-shirt and loose jeans.

Giving myself one last glance in the mirror, I finger comb my hair back. I look like a nice normal guy. Right? Not some pervert who was playing a prank on him. Hopefully, he'll understand. I know I could just blow him off and get on with my life, maybe one day even laugh to myself about how I once sexted with another guy, but all I can come up with is that he deserves more than that.

What would he tell Nora? Would he lay in bed in his underwear, lamenting over his embarrassment? I'm half to blame here. Yeah, I have to tell him in person. I've got this.

JULES

CHAPTER 17

"C'mon Nora! We're gonna be late!" I bellow down the hall.

What the hell is taking her so long? It's not like she's the one with the *coincidate.*

"I'm going to get some work done while I'm there. I can't just sit there and stare at you two making puppy dog eyes at each other the entire time."

"How do I look?" I ask, spinning around to show off my outfit.

I decided to go casual. It's just a coffee shop. Jeans and a green T-shirt. James always said I looked good in green.

"Fine," Nora says, her gaze still fixed on the laptop and paperwork she's packing up.

"Just fine?"

She didn't even look at me. How would she know if I looked just *fine?* Doesn't she know that you don't tell a person that they look *just fine?*

"Okay, you are a beautiful hunk of man meat. Can we go?" she huffs, stuffing her laptop into her bag.

"Yep, but we're walking," I say, grabbing the keys off the hook. "I am not stuffing myself in your *Go-Kart* of a vehicle."

I hate that fucking car. If we took it, my head would be smashed up against the ceiling and ruin my hair. I'm not vain, but I'll bet it's still date code that you don't show up to a first *coincidate* with fucked up hair.

The coffee shop is just a few blocks down the street, and it's a beautiful day. We walk side by side down the sidewalk where neighborhood families are outside enjoying the sunshine. It reminds me of all the walks James and I took together down this very path.

Would he be upset with me for meeting someone? What if Liam doesn't even like me in person? Picking at the hem of my shirt and humming anxiously to myself, Nora interrupts my spinning thoughts.

"Okay, so what's the signal?" she asks.

"*Signal?*"

"Yeah, the signal that you'll give me to let me know he's not a maniac serial killer, so I can go home. I'm not sitting there all day."

"Oh, okay. A signal. Yeah. Good idea. I don't know. What should I do?"

"Pat your head three times, then I'll know I can leave."

"Like this?" I ask while patting the top of my head several times.

"Yeah, but just three times. If you do it like that you'll look like a moron."

Way to sugar coat it for me, Nora. Doesn't she have any idea how nervous and perplexed I am over this entire ordeal?

"Okay. Got it. Only three times."

When we get to the entrance of the coffee shop, I stop outside the door to take a deep breath. This is the first time I've met anyone new with any sort of potential since James died, and it scares the shit out of me. I have to move on at some point, but who knew it would be so damn difficult? So many things have changed since I've been in the dating game. I have no idea what I'm doing.

"I don't think I can do this," I whisper, my hand going still on the coffee shop door. "I feel like I'm gonna throw up," I add, turning around and forcing a deep breath through my nose.

Nope. I can't do this. What the fuck was I thinking?

"Yes, you can Jules," Nora urges, giving my shoulder a squeeze. "This is just a friendly meet-up thing. It *isn't* a date. Remember? Quit psyching yourself out."

"Yeah, but still...." I groan with a sigh.

Am I moving on too fast just by meeting this person? I feel like I'm betraying James even by having a simple coffee with someone else, even if it was someone I hadn't sexted. Seriously, why did I think this was a good idea?

"No, listen to me," she affirms, grabbing my other shoulder now to make me face her, "You're going to go in there and meet this man. You look like a sexy man beast right now. Don't waste it. *You. Got. This,*" she emphasizes, looking me in the eyes and giving me a nod.

I breathe deeply through my nose and exhale loudly, trying to calm down the anxiety working its way through my stomach. Slow deep breaths. I can do this. I won't let these nerves get the best of me. Time to put on my big boy pants.

"Okay. You're right. I can do this," I say, shaking my head to pump myself up to swing the door open.

"I'll go in after you," she whispers, "so we don't look *sus*," she dead-pans, giving me a conspiratorial look.

She should have gone into drama. Rolling my eyes, I walk inside the coffee shop. The aloe plant table is empty, making my heart sink. How can I feel guilty and disappointed at the same time? The clock above the counter indicates I'm five minutes early. Okay. Maybe I'm just the first one here.

Walking up to the counter, I place my normal order, but have a moment of hesitation when the barista asks if I'd like anything else. Am I supposed to get Liam a coffee too? I don't know what he likes. What are the rules to a *coincidate*?

Stammering, I shake my head and pull out my wallet. I'll just offer to buy his coffee when he gets here. Duh, it'd be cold if I bought it now. Christ, I've been out of the game for so long, I don't even know what to do when you go out for coffee with someone.

Carting my cup to my usual seat, I settle in and wait. *Allie the Aloe* is looking just fine today. She's had plenty of water recently judging from her puffy spines. Settling into my seat, I ponder what Liam looks like. How will I know it's him? I didn't get a selfie in return. Did he not like what he saw? Looking up I spot Nora across the café, opening her laptop.

She nods and mouths, "You got this."

I give her a nod in return. I'm a nervous fucking wreck but having her here helps. At least I know I won't get chopped up and tossed in the ocean.

When I hear the bell above the door jingle, I look over at a man making his way inside and to the counter. My mouth gapes open. Swinging my arms as discreetly as I can to Nora, I finally get her attention. Glancing up from her laptop, she frowns at me.

"It's The Tomato Guy," I whisper-yell.

She puts her hands up in confusion, squinting to read my lips and mouths, "What?"

"The—" I mouth but don't get the rest out.

Is Tomato Guy walking over to my table? Oh God, he is. Why did he and his sexy dimple pick today of all days to come over here?

Wait. *No way.*

Is the Tomato Guy...Liam?

That would be too good to be true. The guy with the cutest dimple I have ever seen can't be my *Recycled Person.*

CHAPTER 18

"Jules?" I ask.

Of course, it's Jules. I don't know why I even ask. He's sitting at the table with the aloe plant on it and looks exactly like the guy in the selfie I received an hour ago.

"Uh, yep. That's me. L-iam?" he hesitates.

He has a wild look in his eyes, like he's nervous or scared, or a little bit of both.

I glance around, shifting my feet back and forth. I can do this.

"Uh, yeah. Liam," I repeat, holding out my hand for him to shake.

"Well. Um, hi," he says, shaking my hand and gesturing to the seat across from him.

I chuckle under my breath, "Well, this is a little awkward, isn't it?" I say, sitting down in the seat.

"Yeah, I've never done this before...I mean, met someone like this," he admits.

"Yeah, same here. Um, I guess we can just be awkward together," I let out on a laugh, which gets him to join me. At least I know he has a good sense of humor. We study each other awkwardly for a moment.

"Soooo..." I say, moving my cup around on the table. "I'm not a serial killer," I offer.

"I mean, you don't look like a serial killer or anything, but they never do. Right?" he says, glancing around. "Anyway, I'm glad we're actually meeting up, face to face."

"Yeah, me too, man. It's nice to finally put a face to those texts."

"Yeah. I'm a little nervous. Not gonna lie. I haven't really met anyone since James died...not that this is a date or anything, but you know," he says, correcting himself and picking at a sugar packet in the condiment holder.

"I know I've said it before, but I'm sorry you lost him. My mother... well, I won't talk about that..."

I know no matter what I say, it won't make him feel better. I've seen grief firsthand, and even though you think you're helping someone by saying something encouraging, you're not.

"No, go ahead," he insists. "It's okay."

"Well, you know, she hasn't been with anyone since my dad passed. It's been hard to see her alone like that for all these years. I'm just happy to see that you're getting out. I would hate for you to never meet any-one again. I've seen what that does to a person," I say, speaking at the surface of the table in front of me.

I feel like such an asshole right now. I hate to do this to him. For whatever reason, I care about his feelings, and I don't want to smash them to bits. He's thinking this is a date. What I need to say is probably going to hurt him and make him bolt out of here in embarrassment. It will be worse than when he realized someone was reading his heartache texts to James.

"Anyway, let's not talk about sad stuff." I clear my throat and force a smile. "So, uh, does Nora have you watching any movies this weekend?"

"Yeah, what's the one with those two dumb guys? We watched that one last night." He snickers.

"A classic!" I bellow, slapping my hand against the table. "I love that one."

I've got to tell him. I'm stalling. The longer we go on like this the harder it's going to be. Time to get my game face on.

"So, Jules...um, here's the thing...I'm not sure what you're really expecting from this, but," I start to say, cowardly looking down at the table again.

"Oh, no. I'm not expecting anything at all," he says, putting his hands up defensively.

"Okay, because well, this is kind of embarrassing, but, um, I'm not... well, *not gay*," I murmur.

"Excuse me?" He gapes.

"I...thought your name was short for *Julie,*" I admit, chuckling under my breath nervously. It's not funny, but my brain doesn't seem to know how to handle what's happening.

"You thought...you thought...oh my God." He claps his hand over his mouth, his eyes going wide.

"Yeah, and I'm totally fucking embarrassed right now," I admit.

"*You're* embarrassed? Holy shit. We...oh God...we—"

"Sexted," I say, finishing his sentence.

Suddenly, I let out a roar of laughter that surprises even me, making his head rear back. Luckily, a second later, he starts laughing along with me, which sets off a chain reaction. We end up in a fit of hysterics.

Phew. At least we can joke about this. I'm so happy he isn't heart-broken and upset. Man or woman, Jules is a special person, even I can see that.

I look up at him, tears streaming down my cheeks, and see him patting his head repeatedly.

"Are you okay? What's wrong with your head?" I ask, which makes him laugh harder, if that was even possible.

"Nothing. Nothing," he says between gasps. "Just, uh, had something in my hair."

Composing myself as our laughter fades, I'm so happy this went better than I expected. As always, I feel like I can be honest with Jules, so I shoot for honesty.

"Yeah, about the sexting. Um...I'd be lying if I said I didn't have... hopes that this could turn into...something, but that was before I saw your picture. I'm really sorry about all this," I reiterate. "I never would have encouraged or led you on, if I knew—"

"No! No, I understand. You're not gay. Got it."

"I'm not...I'm not against that or anything. I don't want you to think that I am," I add.

I'm not homophobic. I won't let him think that. I've just never... well...been with a man before.

93

"Wow. Yeah. Thanks for saying that," he says, sitting back in his chair.

"I just didn't want you to think I was homophobic or anything, totally not," I assure him.

"This is so crazy. I don't think I've ever been mistaken for a woman before," he jokes, his head in his hands.

"Well, no, you definitely don't look like a woman. If I were gay, I'd say you're an attractive dude," I admit, trying to make him feel better.

He is a good-looking guy, even I can admit that. I bet the guys go wild for him.

"*So, you're saying there's a chance?*" he teases, a huge smile on his face.

I let out a loud laugh. I can't stop laughing around this guy.

"Did you just.... *Dumb and Dumber* me?"

*****

We get out of the stuffy café and agree on taking a walk. Jules is right. It's a beautiful day. The sun is shining, and the whole town seems to be out, wandering around the small downtown area.

I glance over at Jules next to me as he talks about Nora. Obviously, she's his best friend and has been there for him through his most difficult times. Thinking about how she got to be there for him leaves an odd feeling in the pit of my stomach. I almost mistake it for jealousy, but that can't be it. I've never felt jealous over a man, much less one I've just met.

"You and Nora are just..."

"Friends," he says, getting straight to the point.

"You've never?" I ask, tilting my head to the side.

He scoffs and starts laughing. "Absolutely not. Nora likes women, and as you've learned...I am not that," he says, moving his hand over his body.

"No. You definitely aren't a woman," I admit.

Because unlike everyone else, I really did learn that the hard way.

"So, this is my place," he says, stopping in the middle of the sidewalk.

"Yeah? I live right over there, about three blocks down," I say, pointing down the road. "I'm surprised we haven't run into each other before."

"Actually, we have," he says, looking at me with a gleam in his eye.

94

"What? We have? When?"

I look him over, trying to place where I may have seen him. I really don't remember meeting him before this.

"You're The Tomato Guy!" he says, cracking up, running his hand over his mouth sheepishly for some reason.

"The tomato...what?"

I really need clarification on this one. I don't know anything about tomatoes.

"I actually saw you at the coffee shop once. Then I met you at the farmer's market. I was so nervous that I made a terrible joke about tomatoes. Honestly, I'm glad you don't remember," he says, shaking his head.

"Oh my God! The *ketchup joke*!" I yell and start laughing again.

Because evidently, all I do is laugh around this guy. Damnit. Why did he have to be a guy?

"Yeah, I'm the ketchup-joke-guy. I, uh, I thought you were cute," he says, shrugging. "And when I'm nervous, I make bad jokes about tomatoes, apparently."

"You thought I was...cute?"

I'm sure I sound insecure as hell, but I'm flattered. Jules thinks I'm cute. It gives me a funny feeling in my stomach, a lot like that feeling when he texted, asking what I was wearing.

"Um, have you seen yourself?" He points at me. "As Nora would say, you're a *delicious hunk of man meat,* and considering that's coming from a lesbian, you know you can probably add like ten points to the man meat meter. Actually, do you want to meet the legend? She's right inside," he says, gesturing toward the door.

"Yeah, I kind of do, since I've heard so much about her."

I do want to meet Nora, but I also don't want to leave him yet. His charisma is kind of addictive. I'm enjoying his company more than I thought I would. He makes me laugh like no one has in a long time. Nothing's changed. He just…has a penis. Why does that make me think about my penis?

We walk up the stairs to his apartment, and for some reason, I'm in the lead. I turn around and look at him, wondering if he's checking out my ass since my placement on the stairs puts it right in front of his face. He bounces ahead of me happily, accidentally brushing against my side. That barest of contact of his warm skin to mine, breaks my arm out into goosebumps.

What the hell was that? Is it because my body remembers we sexted?

When we finally get to his front door, I look into his eyes, trying to get some type of read on him, seeing if he felt that too. That weird prickly sensation.

He winks at me as he opens the door. "And here she is!" he says, announcing Nora's presence in the living room. She's sprawled out on the couch, staring at her laptop with her hand in a big bowl of popcorn.

"Jules! Just you? Well, at least you have some more images for your spank bank," she yells across the room.

Chuckling at her joke, I pivot a little to the right to make myself known.

"Nora! It's The Tomato Guy! And he isn't gay! Can you believe it?" Jules sputters out.

He seems almost happy about the fact that I'm not gay. Why is he so happy about it? Why does it bother me that he's happy about it?

I barely make it through the doorway of their little apartment before Nora barrels off the couch and starts toward me.

"Liam? *This* is Liam? And he's *also* The Tomato Guy? What the hell are the chances of that?" she says, moving her hands around rapidly. "Holy crap!" she squeals, clapping her hands together.   I walk a few steps into the house to introduce myself to her when a very plump cat makes an appearance. He ambles over to me slowly and rubs against the side of my leg, letting out a loud purr. I bend down, rubbing under the chin that he's displayed for me.

"And who is this?" I ask, looking up at two shocked faces.

"That's...Fishsticks...and he...and he..." Nora stammers, as though she can't form words.

"What's up Fishsticks?" I say, looking down at the fat orange specimen in front of me.

He gives me an adorable meow in return. Glancing over at Jules, I find an identical shocked expression. What's going on here?

"What?" I ask.

"*Fishsticks likes you!*" he exclaims. "Fishsticks doesn't like *anyone*!"

Glancing down, I see Fishsticks purring at my feet, belly up. I make my way down to him slowly and give him a light stroke to his belly.

"*Oh. My. God. A belly rub!*" Nora practically screams, putting her hand over her mouth.

"How are you doing that? Fishsticks is the spawn of Satan! He hates the entire world!" Jules blurts out.

I don't know what the commotion is all about. It's just a cat, a cat that seems incredibly friendly and full of love.

"I've heard so much about you," I say, standing up and putting out my hand, officially introducing myself to Nora.

"I would say the same about you, but not really," she says sarcastically.

I like her already. There's nothing more I appreciate than some good quality sarcasm, plus, I know I shouldn't, but I like the idea that Jules gabbed about me.

"So, you're not gay? That's what I just heard, right?" she asks, raising an eyebrow.

"Yeah, not gay. Sorry."

"It was a huge misunderstanding, Nora. I'll tell you later...no big deal though, right?" he says, looking in my direction.

"Right. No big deal," I respond, putting my hands up in front of me in surrender.

It is kind of a big deal, but I'm glad Jules isn't making it one. I could totally understand if he did. I mean, he thought I was a man.

"That's too bad. Jules here was having the hots for you at the farmer's market," she says, elbowing him in the side.

I let out a snort. I can feel my face reddening with embarrassment.

Fuck, did I just snort?

"I didn't deny that," he jeers at her. "I already told him, so nice try on embarrassing me."

"Wow, it's like you're an adult today," she exclaims.

"Well, I don't want to impose," I interject. "I should probably get going..."

I feel awkward right now and completely out of my element. I've been out with Oscar enough that I know how to socialize with strangers. Today? Why is it so difficult. This never happens to me. What happened to the cool Liam? That Liam has shown himself out and in has come embarrassed Liam with a peculiar feeling in his chest.

"Oh, okay," Jules says with a smile.

He has a great smile. His lip curls up, leaving a row of straight white teeth.

"It was nice meeting you Nora, and you too Jules. Can I call you Julian? Well, because you know..." I laugh nervously.

If I call him *Jules*, I will forever be reminded of this huge embarrassing mix-up.

He smirks at me. "Yeah, definitely. Julian it is."

JULES

CHAPTER 19

"So. He's *not gay*?" Nora asks as soon as Liam walks out of the door.

"Nope," I concur.

I won't say that I'm not disappointed about it. I am. I really liked him when we were texting. And that sexting we did? Hot as hell. It makes me wonder how good he is in bed.

I made a huge step today. Even though Liam isn't gay, I got myself out there. I willingly went out to meet another human being. I'm proud of myself. None of it was as bad as I thought it would be. The guilt I thought I would feel over James? Also, not as bad as I thought it would be. Even though I lost the prospect of ever possibly dating Liam, I still won a little bit.

"You sure about that?" she asks, an eyebrow raised.

"Well, yeah. You heard him. He just told us he isn't gay. Am I supposed to think he was lying about that?"

"The way he looked at you though, you didn't notice that?" she questions, squinting her eyes at me.

"Notice what?"

I didn't notice a thing. Sure, I was attracted to the guy, and I admitted it to him. But he's not gay. There's no changing that. He seems like someone I could at least be friends with though. It would be nice to have a friend aside from Nora.

"He just, never mind." She sighs. "*Not gay*. Got it. How did it go otherwise? Are you going to keep in touch?" she asks, taking a seat back on the couch.

"Yeah, maybe. I mean, I was hoping he was gay obviously, because look at him, but yeah. Maybe we'll keep in touch as friends? I'm not sure. We didn't really address it."

I hope we can keep being text friends, at the very least. I truly do, but I definitely shouldn't text him first. I don't want to come across like I'm hitting on him. If he wants to keep texting, he can let me know. I'd love to hear from him again, but if I don't, I completely understand. I mean, the guy thought he was going on a date with a woman.

"Hm," Nora hums, unpausing her movie.

"What's that? What's *hmmm*?"

"Did you see how Fishsticks reacted to him?"

"Yeah. What the hell was that about? I've never seen him like anyone but James."

She throws up her hands and scoffs. "That's *all* I'm going to say!"

Is she implying Liam would have to be a serial killer after all if Fishsticks liked him? I'm not in the mood to dampen the image I have of him now that we've met. I've barely just processed that he's straight. Ha! Just my luck. At least he was as cool straight as he was gay. No way am I going to let her ruin that with one of her wild hypotheses.

"Okay, whatever," I grumble, making my way to my room. "I can't understand your weird mind. It's as mad as a March hare!"

Dropping onto my bed, I put in my earbuds. Sometimes listening to audiobooks helps me get in the mood to write. Maybe I'll get lucky after this strange day and find some inspiration. I turn on a romance I had been listening to about two guys who hate each other but end up together in the end. The sex is always so hot in enemies-to-lovers stories, so it should be a nice mindless distraction from reality.

A sex scene starts and within seconds, Liam has replaced my image of the main character in my head. His defined jaw that I'd love to trail kisses down. His dirty blonde hair that I'd like to run my hands through. His fucking dimple. We're not enemies like in this book. I know he's straight, but damn, listening to a spicier version of what we sexted about, I can't help but imagine what could happen if he wasn't.

The things he said that day…

I lean over to my nightstand without a second thought. Opening the drawer, I find the bottle of lube. It's not like he'll know, and it's not like I'm cheating on James if it's just a fantasy. Right? It's perfect, if you think about it. Maybe Nora was right. I've at least added a few images to my lonely spank bank.

Slickening up my cock, I imagine Liam's lean muscles, his defined arms with that sexy tattoo. Is it weird that I kind of want to lick that tattoo? I don't think I ever licked James. We were pretty vanilla, and I was perfectly content with that. Liam though? When I think of Liam I want…I want to do all the things…

Blood immediately rushes to my groin, tightening up my balls. My cock is rock hard in my hand, my balls arching and begging for more. I strengthen my grip, imagining what Liam would look like on top of me, his lips around me, sucking me off.

Fuck.

I stifle a moan, picturing his head bobbing up and down, his hands playing with my balls while he stares up at me. God, what I wouldn't give for Liam to be gay.

I grip my cock tighter, my hand moving faster and faster with each image that pops into my head. I could imagine him doing so many dirty things to me. And wait just a minute, I would be totally okay with Liam doing filthy things to me? Maybe I'm doing better than I realized.

I come with a loud moan. My release rocks through me so hard, thick ribbons arc through the air and land on my belly and my chest. Practically melting into the bed, it takes a good five minutes to regain my breath.

Holy shit.

I just jacked myself into a mind-blowing orgasm while fantasizing about a straight man that I just met. I have absolutely no shame.

LIAM

CHAPTER 20

He thinks...I'm cute?

I don't know why that part of the whole day has stuck with me, but it has.

Julian thinks I'm cute.

I switch on the TV, unable to concentrate on work, or anything for that matter. The day was a whirlwind. I mindlessly scroll through *Netflix,* hoping something will distract me from my feelings.

I end up clicking on something I don't even care about, my brain too busy reliving what went on between Julian and I today. I expected him to freak out and run off once he found out I wasn't gay, but he took the whole thing in stride. It makes me respect him more than I already did.

And he made me laugh in person even more than he did in his texts. I hate to admit this to myself, but I don't think I've ever laughed like that. And...the way my body reacted when he brushed passed me? The way my stomach did that weird flip thing when we were talking at the coffee shop? What the hell was that all about?

THE RIGHT WRONG NUMBER

Do I...think Julian is...cute too? Like the way he thinks I'm cute?

I assumed I couldn't get him out of my mind all day because it was new, seeing his face was new, but now I'm not so sure. Every time I see him in my mind's eye, that stomach flip thing happens again. Closing my eyes, I imagine his face, his brown hair that's just a little too long. His blue eyes that are sad but also full of hope.

Okay, yeah. He's handsome. I can admit that. I'm enough of a man to admit that I can appreciate a good-looking person, no matter their gender. Does that make me like, attracted to him though?

Leaning forward, I grab my phone off the coffee table. I should let him know I'm still here for him. It doesn't matter that we ended up not completely being who we thought we were. I mean, we still had all that connection over the last few weeks, regardless of anatomy. We shared things, pieces of ourselves, of our lives. I feel like that meant something to him just as much as it did to me, otherwise we wouldn't have gotten on so well today and gotten over the gender mix up so easily. Smiling, I type out a silly joke I remember hearing a kid tell his mom at a grocery store.

What's broccoli's favorite type of music?

Perfect. He's going to love it. I know it. Especially after that tomato joke he made at the farmer's market.

Man, I can't believe I didn't connect that it was him at the farmer's market that day. The memory of our exchange and his silly behavior that day has me chuckling. He freaking mentioned Nora buying some crap, and I didn't even pick up on it until now. Oh, Julian. How could anybody not like the guy? Is that what my stomach flipping thing is about?

I like women, but then again, being with a man has never really crossed my mind. I do what I saw around me growing up, which is men being with women. And yes, I can say for certain that I like women. I've only been with women, and my cock reacts positively to them.

But *wait, wait, wait.* Maybe that's what I need to ask myself?

Does...my cock react to Julian?

Glancing down at my lap, I reach down and rub my cock up and down through my jeans. It's already half-mast.

Shit. Okay, well, I mean, I was just thinking about sleeping with women. Of course it's at attention.

Julian. Right. Think about Julian. This is just a test.

Easily, I recall the images that haven't left me, except this time, I imagine him without a shirt on, and with the hard abs that I assume might be under it. The tiny trail of hair that might peek out above his jeans. I picture him in black boxer briefs, lying on his bed like he probably did that day we sexted, except I imagine I'm standing at the end of his bed this time.

I need to make this real if I want to find out. It occurs to me that he was hard that day, like really occurs to me in my visual. Another man was hard for me. I made Julian hard for me just by talking to him. I picture an image of him breathing heavily on his bed, want in his eyes, his cock straining against the fabric of his boxers.

Holy shit.

My cock bucks behind my jeans violently. My length is now rock hard, completely full of need behind the denim.

I shove my jeans just down past my ass and pull out my length, hot and hard against my abs, wanting to see the proof, wanting to show it off proudly to him. I look up, and Julian is still in front of me, taking out his own cock, giving it a long stroke. I follow his lead, tightening my hand around myself, giving myself a long lazy stroke just like he did.

He licks his lips while looking into my eyes, almost egging me on.

"Yes," I mutter as he grabs himself, stroking himself harder.

I time my movements with him. Stroking faster, then slower. His hand goes down, stroking his balls, running his finger along his taint. It's a dare, a battle, and my body wants to be an equal adversary. I do the same, matching him move for move.

"Keep going," he whispers, "come for me."

I pick up my speed, hips jerking into my hand, unable to control myself any longer. My balls are heavy, my cock so hard it's almost painful. Why is this so erotic, so potent?

I watch him intensively, trying to wait for him. I just can't hang on any longer. My hand moves faster, spine straightening up, sending shocks throughout my body. With a loud groan, I shudder, coming on my chest, my stomach, and my hand. My head hits the back of the couch.

When I look up, Julian's gone. I feel the loss of him immediately, wanting him to come back to my imagination, to be a part of my fantasy.

When I look down at my release that covers my stomach, reality sets in. I just came to a fantasy of Julian, and my cock very much liked the idea of him.

The sound of my phone getting a notification stops my frantic thoughts.

Julian? Please be Julian.

I hurry up and grab it off the coffee table, seeing just one word on the screen.

JULES: What?

I laugh, remembering my last text to him. Oh yeah, the broccoli.

ME: Brock 'n roll.

A second later, another notification comes through.

JULES: I'll remember that one next time I hit on a cute guy at the farmer's market.

Um, the next time...he what?

JULES

CHAPTER 21

Nora and I have been fighting with Fishsticks for over an hour attempting to give him his insulin. Turns out, insulin must be given into the back of the neck. In order to avoid injury, I'm decked out in my heaviest coat and oven mitts. I'm sweating my ass off. I think Dr. Theo had the right idea with welding gloves. Can I order some off *Amazon?* Nora is wearing a freaking colander on her head like Fishsticks might have the audacity to claw up her skull. I wouldn't put it past him. The way Fishsticks slides out of our arms when we try to catch him makes him look like a gold medal Olympian gymnast. A pill in his food would have been way easier than this. You'd think we're dealing with a circus trained cat.

"What are we supposed to do?" I ask Nora, taking a seat at the dining room table. "There has got to be a better way."

"My next covert operation are these bad boys!" she exclaims, holding up a huge canister of cat treats.

The exact same kind James used to give him. The kind that Nora said he couldn't have any more because he was on a diet.

"You've sunk low," I snort.

"Listen, if you have any other ideas, please feel free to let me know. I am fresh out."

"Alright, let's let him chill out for a bit, and then we'll break out the top-notch goods."

We move over to the couch to put on a movie, one of Nora's picks, of course. I never get to pick the movies around here.

"*Dirty Dancing* again?" I mutter.

We've seen this a million times. Nora has a Patrick Swayze fetish. I won't lie about the fact that I might have one too. I mean, if you deny to me that you don't like Patrick Swayze, I will automatically determine that we can't be friends. Because you're a fucking liar.

"Don't even deny how much you love gawking at Patrick Swayze without a shirt."

"I would never deny such a thing," I admit, laying down on the opposite side of the couch and resting my feet on her lap.

"Get your feet off me! Damnit, don't you ever wear socks?" she says, swatting her hand at me.

"Socks are like little tiny prisons for my feet," I say, sticking my foot in her face.

"Ugh! You're gross!" she grunts, smacking my feet away.

I put my foot down only because Patrick Swayze has made his appearance. My phone dings on the coffee table, interrupting my Swayze-staring. Picking up my phone with one hand, I see Liam's name on the screen. The Liam I had sexual fantasies about last night. My cock twitches under my sweatpants at the thought of it.

LIAM: What's the coolest vegetable?

I see how it is. He will never let me live the tomato joke down. Fine. I'll let him have his fun.

ME: I dunno. What?

Without a chance to put my phone down, he replies.

LIAM: A radish!

I bark out a laugh, looking over at Nora to see if she noticed. She didn't. She's too wrapped up in watching *Baby* try to carry watermelons. Turns out, Nora has a *Baby* fetish.

ME: Hilarious.

LIAM: What are you up to?

ME: Attempting to give Fishsticks his insulin. Turns out he has diabetes.

LIAM: *Diabetus.*

ME: Yes, Wilford Brimley. And giving Fishsticks his insulin is difficult because he's a demon.

I look over and find Fishsticks sleeping under the dining room table, snoring like a grown ass man. He's got his dirty sock tucked under his paw. I wish I could find a way to get it away from him and wash it. I look like I don't take care of my cat with that filthy thing hanging out of his mouth every day.

LIAM: Don't say that about him! He was quite the gentleman when I met him!

ME: I guess you're special.

LIAM: Damn right I am.

Nora notices me texting someone, a look of shenanigans in her eyes. The minute she side-eyes me, I know she's up to no good.

"Whatever it is, no."

"I was just thinking—"

"That's scary," I interrupt.

"Funny. You're hilarious, Jules. What if...now hear me out, what if we ask Liam to come over to help us with Fishsticks?" she asks with a hopeful look.

"No," I say bluntly.

I'm not texting him and asking him to come over here. I don't want him to think I'm coming onto him. And asking him to come over to my place? Yeah, sounds like I'm making a move. I want to be his friend, not scare him off.

She shrugs, deciding to drop the subject and get back to her movie. I look back down at my phone. Smirking, I read the last text. Fishsticks is right. Liam is special. He gets me and my weird sense of humor, and I want to keep the conversation going, so I shoot off another text.

ME: I'm sure Fishsticks would like to see you again.

Maybe Nora is right. If Liam and I become friends, he can help us with Fishsticks. Not that I would expect that, but it would be nice to have a reprieve from tackling a twenty-five-pound cat twice a day.

LIAM: If you need help with him, just let me know. How is Nora?

ME: Watching *Dirty Dancing*. I'm not complaining.

LIAM: I figured Nora was a *Dirty Dancing* fan.

LIAM: You have anything going on tonight? Was thinking about having a drink after work? Wanna meet up?

Huh, just friends having a beer, right? Or am I trying to read into something that isn't even there? I like this man, like—I *like like* him. I mean, I've had sexual fantasies about him. We can't be anything more than friends, and I really need to accept that. He's straight, and I'm still in love with my dead husband. He's not coming onto me as much as my cock wants him to. He wants to be friends, and if having Liam as a friend is all I can get, I'll take it.

ME: Sure. When? Where?

LIAM: *Mixers* at 6?

ME: I'll meet you there.

"Who ya' talking to over there?" Nora asks, while still staring at the TV.

"Liam. He invited me out for a drink tonight."

Nora side-eyes me again. "Huh," she grunts.

"What?" I mutter, looking over at her.

She shakes her head, "Nothing."

"You have nothing to say? That's shocking," I retort. "I'm gonna jump in the shower."

I strip down and get under the hot scalding water, still thinking about Liam. He has occupied all my thoughts lately with James moving over to the side. If this little mix up has taught me anything, it's that moving on is definitely plausible.

Liam is straight. *He's straight. He's straight.* I repeat it to myself like a mantra. I need to remind myself that nothing can come of this. Having a crush on a straight man will do me no good. It will only lead to a broken heart, and my heart has been broken enough for a lifetime.

CHAPTER 22

LIAM: I'm here.

I walk up to the half-empty bar, waving down the bartender. I'm going for a *Jack* and *Coke* tonight. Not my normal, but I need something to take the edge off. I look around the small bar. It's a Tuesday night, which means it's quieter than normal. No loud jukebox in the background, and a quiet after-work crowd that's just looking to have a drink before they make their way home.

Sitting down, I swing around in my barstool nervously. Why am I nervous? Deep inside my gut, I know exactly why I'm nervous. I just can't admit that to myself, not right now. Not yet.

I remind myself that I'm here to meet Julian as a friend. *Just as a friend.* After my little fantasy, my feelings are all mashed together in my chest, spinning around inside of me like a blender. I'm disorientated and muddled. I'm here to see Julian again and maybe try and sort out what's going on inside me, so I can move onto a friendship with him, that's all.

Pulling my phone out of my pocket to check the time, I see a text from him.

JULES: Be there in 5.

Which came in...four minutes ago.

My eyes dart to the door every few seconds, knowing he's about to walk through. When it opens and he walks in, my breath hitches a little. I wave him over, letting him know where I'm sitting.

I watch as he saunters in my direction, giving me a half wave and a small smile. A cute half wave and a cute half smile.

Fuck.

When he sits down next to me, I can feel his body heat radiating off him. It's rubbing off on me, making me feel all hot and bothered. Yes, it's definitely just his body heat. That's all.

"Hey, man," he says nonchalantly, bumping my shoulder as he positions himself in the barstool next to me.

Of course, we would end up being this close. We're sitting at a bar for Christ's sake. Maybe I should have chosen a table, with ya know, a larger space between us.

"How's it going? Did Fishsticks get his medicine?" I ask.

"Yeah, Nora got his favorite cat treats. She's got some tricks up her sleeve," he says with a laugh.

"Yeah, she sure seems like it. I like her. She seems like fun," I note while taking a swig of my drink.

Nora and Julian seem to have a perfect friendship, the exact opposite of me and Oscar. It's a little sad that my only friend is a major douche canoe.

Julian studies me, looking me up and down, giving me a strange look. "I told you she likes women, right? You didn't just invite me here to try to get into her good graces, did you?" He questions me with a laugh but also with a touch of sadness in his eyes.

He thinks I'm here for his best friend? If he only knew who has actually been on my mind.

"No. You told me she was gay. I'm not attracted to her...I," I stutter.

What I really want to say is that I'm attracted to *him*, but there's no way I can say that. My mouth won't let me form those words. Those things can apparently only occur in my fantasies.

"Oh. Okay. Gotcha. Just making sure," he adds, a small smile on his face.

The bartender finally makes his way over, asking Julian what he'd like to drink. He orders a beer, and I motion for the bartender to send another *Jack* and *Coke* my way.

"Rough day?" Julian asks, gesturing to my empty glass. "What do you do exactly?"

"I code. It's a lot of numbers, and, well, boring. Yeah, rough day."

Not rough for the reasons he thinks though. Work has nothing to do with the way I'm feeling right now.

"Ah, I'm a writer, or I *was* a writer. I haven't really had anything going on in that department since James died. I'm working on it. Getting there," he says, tapping the side of his head.

"That's really awesome. I'd love to read your work. What have you written? Would I know of it?" I ask excitedly.

I'm sure he hears that a lot when he tells people he's a writer, but I am interested. I'd like to get a look into that head of his.

He chortles. "No, definitely not. I write gay romantic comedies, which I'm sure isn't your thing."

"Hey, never know, right? I'm going to look up one of your books, I swear," I add, holding up my hand like I'm taking an oath.

He looks up and takes a swig of his beer. His lips wrap around the beer bottle, and I can't help but wonder what they feel like beneath my fingers. What they might feel like against my own lips. How his tongue would feel, pushing its way into my mouth. How it would feel licking all the parts he said he wanted to lick when we sexted.

"What's with this tattoo?" he asks, pointing at my forearm, interrupting my overwhelming thoughts.

Ah, my tattoo. I hide it the best I can with my long-sleeved shirts, but mostly so I can look presentable. I was young and dumb, and even though I get a lot of comments on how cool it looks, it's something I regret now that I'm older, especially now that I work in an office.

"Ah, that...weren't we all young once?" I chuckle, trying to change the subject.

He leans over just slightly, rubbing a finger gently along the cuff of my sleeve. His touch sends a tingle straight up my spine.

"I like it," he states, and gauging by the way he says it, he has no idea what that simple touch has just done to me.

"Julian," I whisper, my voice coming out huskier than normal.

I clear my throat over the massive lump that sits there. My hands won't stop fidgeting back and forth, which makes my barstool move in his direction just slightly. Our legs touch, sending a path of goosebumps down my arms. I quickly move my leg back into my own space.

Shit. Why did I pick the stools and not a table?

"You alright?" he asks, bending his head down just enough to look me in the eyes.

I look the other direction, trying to avoid eye contact. My gaze draws back to him, making me acutely aware of him in a different way. His gaze holds onto mine making it so I can barely get my words out.

"Uh, yeah...yeah...sorry...just uh," I stutter, "I should go..."

"Oh. Um. Okay," he says, looking rightly confused, especially considering I asked him to meet me and he just got here. "Yeah, you look like you had a long day."

I gulp down what's left of my drink and stand up. "Thanks for coming for the drink," I say, tilting my glass in his direction. "You going to stick around?"

He looks around the bar warily. "Um, yeah. I'll just finish this one, I guess."

"Okay. Yeah. Okay," I say, glancing around, seeing if there's anyone he's looking at.

Is he checking someone out while he's with me? Not that I even have a say in if he checks someone out. I can't even say what's going on in my head out loud. How could I expect him to not check someone else out?

I head for the door, giving him one last look before I walk out. I don't like the idea of leaving him here alone, of him possibly looking for someone else to share a conversation with, a conversation I should be having with him.

Walking down the street to my apartment, I stop in my tracks, debating on if I should go back. I shouldn't have left like that. I fucked up. I'm not sure what's going on here, but I do know this fiery feeling in the pit of my stomach. It's jealousy.

JULES

CHAPTER 23

What the fuck...was that? I can't say that I know Liam enough to know if something was off about him, but he sure seemed off. Maybe it was like he said, he had a rough day at work, and that's all it was.

I twirl the top of my beer bottle with my fingers. I haven't been out to a bar in over a year, and now that I'm here, I'm here alone. Fantastic.

The bartender approaches me, asking if I'd like another. Screw it. I'm already here. Let's make it two. He pops the cap off a beer and slides it my way, immediately walking away to tend to someone else.

I've been to this bar before with James, since it's right down the street from our apartment. It hasn't changed much in the last year. A fancy new digital jukebox has replaced the old one. The walls are still the same, old wood panels that have neon beer signs on them. Nothing fancy, but kind of homey just the same.

I yank my phone out of my pocket, determined to make myself look busy to the people around me. There's nothing creepier than a guy sitting alone at a bar staring at people. I debate texting Nora, see if she wants to keep me company for my last beer when I sense a presence behind me. Looking up and swinging my barstool around, I see a guy dressed in a suit standing to my right.

"What's up?" he asks, taking a seat beside me. "Waiting on someone?"

"Nah, my buddy just left. Just finishing up my beer. Can't waste it," I answer with a chuckle.

"Name's Brandon," he says, sticking out his hand for me to shake.

"Jules," I respond, shaking his hand.

He's kind of sexy. Not like Liam sexy, but still sexy. He's got this laid-back vibe about him. Short brown hair, shaved on the sides with a clean-cut goatee.

Taking a swig of my beer, I look back over at him. "Stressful day?" I ask, trying to make conversation.

"Yeah, same old same old," he says, holding up his beer. "You?"

"Could have been better," I answer.

Because really, it could have. What the hell just happened? I figured Liam would have stayed for at least half an hour, not ten minutes, and then end up running out of here like he was being chased by a rabid dog.

"I've never seen you around here before," Brandon muses.

"Nah, I don't get out as much as I used to," I reply.

I don't, and honestly, looking around this place I can easily figure out why. This just isn't my thing anymore. Sure, I had fun in the bars when I was younger, but as a thirty-six-year-old, hangovers are a bitch. The bars are loud and let's face it, people are obnoxious when they're drunk. I just don't have the patience for it anymore.

My new friend Brandon keeps talking, droning on and on about something, but I just tune him out. He's talking about his work, maybe? I have no clue at this point, so I nod my head every once in a while, making it seem like I'm paying attention. My mind can't stop drifting back to Liam.

Shit. Did I do something wrong?

I gulp down the rest of my beer and start to stand up. "Well, nice to meet you, Brandon," I say, giving him a nod.

I lay down a twenty for the bartender when I feel a hand on my shoulder. My new friend Brandon is stopping me from leaving, and I'm not a fan of it.

"Hold on, wait," he says.

I stare at his hand on my shoulder, silently begging for him to get it off me. He grabs a napkin off the bar and scribbles a phone number on it before handing it to me.

"Here," he says, winking. "In case you ever, want to have fun. Or something."

Wow. He's implying casual sex. He may be kind of sexy, but I'm not interested.

"Thanks," I say, grabbing the napkin to be polite. "I'll give you a call sometime," I lie.

I'm never calling this man. Thinking about having casual sex with him makes me want to dry heave.

When I finally make it home, I shove my key in the lock quietly, trying not to wake Nora. Taking two steps in and looking around, I find her wide-awake sitting in the dark, jabbing away at her laptop.

"How'd it go?" she asks, glancing over her screen.

"Um. I don't really know. Liam just kind of...left," I answer. "And some guy gave me his number," I add, holding up the napkin.

"He just...left?"

"Yeah, it was odd. I don't know. He looked tired, I guess," I answer with a shrug.

"Are you going to call him?" she asks, pointing to the napkin in my hand.

"Who? Oh. Nope. Not a chance," I mutter, tossing the napkin in the garbage.

Shrugging off my coat, I pull my phone out of my pocket and see Liam's name on the screen. I swipe the message open.

LIAM: Sorry. Just a rough day.

Okay.

I type back, hitting send.

I'm tired. My brain has been moving around at warp speeds, and I just need it to shut up already. I head to my room to get reacquainted with my favorite friend, my mattress. He's never let me down.

"Night, Nora," I call on my way.

"Good night. Horrible dreams!"

Ha. Horrible dreams. My best friend in the whole wide world wishes I have horrible dreams. I mean, it seems fitting for the week I've had. I don't need to have horrible dreams. I can just replay the past few days.

CHAPTER 24

It was a long, confusing week, so I decided to go out with Oscar tonight. For the first time in history, I asked him. He thinks I'm here to look for a hook-up to take the edge off a rough work week. He is so fucking wrong.

I'm not here to check out women like Oscar believes. I'm here to check out men. I can't quite figure out where these feelings for Julian have come from. I've never been attracted to a man in my life. I even went as far as watching gay porn, which did...well, absolutely nothing. I mean, I thought about how it would feel if I did that with Julian and had to have a round with my hand. But all the guys I saw on the screen? A big nope from me, I saw a lot of them.

"Earth to Liam," Oscar says, waving his hand in front of my face. "Where'd you just go?"

"Huh. Oh. Just spacing out. Tired I guess," I reply with a sigh.

"How's things with Jules? The text-message-girl? Anything happen with that?" Oscar asks with a wink.

"No. Yeah. Well, we met. It went okay," I admit.

"You had a *sext-scapade,* and it just went, *okay?*" he says, drawing out the last word sarcastically.

"Yeah, I like...um...her," I stutter over the last word.

The *her* part of that sentence almost tripped me up. I don't need Oscar's shit right now, and I don't even know what the hell is going on with Julian, so I'm not going to bring it up. The less Oscar knows about this, the better.

"Must be a bust by how unexcited you sound," he says with a laugh. "That girl, two o'clock, looks like she wouldn't be a bust," he says, nudging my foot under the table.

"You know you can just say *left or right* like a normal person?" I growl, turning around in my chair.

I'm not looking at the girl though. I'm looking for a man, any man for my eyes to land on.

"Cute, huh? Her ass in that dress though? *Phew,*" he whistles, looking to my side.

"Yeah, definitely," I mutter.

I'm pretending to look at the woman, when I'm actually looking at the man to her left. I study him, noticing his build, the way he smiles, and he's, well...*not* Julian. He does nothing for me. Not a spark of excitement. Not a cock twitch. Nothing. Per the usual.

I look back at Oscar. "What about you? Anyone you talking to?" I ask, changing the subject.

"You know me...they don't hang around long." He snickers like he's a player or something.

No, Oscar. They don't hang around long because you're an asshole.

"I'm going to get another," I say. Making my way to the bar, my eyes move around the room for another man that might make me feel...something.

I saddle up to the bar, giving the bartender a wave. I happen to be standing next to a guy in a green shirt with close cut brown hair. I glance over casually, trying not to make it obvious that I'm looking at him.

"Hey, do I know you?" he asks.

Shit. He noticed me looking at him. Fuck.

"Nah, just waiting on the bartender. He's a little backed up," I mutter, trying to make it look like that's what I'm really doing.

"I think I saw you in here the other day," he states. "Brandon," he adds.

"Yeah, I come in here sometimes," I mutter.

This time I look at him, *really* look at him. He's got a short, maintained goatee, and an earring in one ear. I give him a once over, and nope, still nothing happening. No goosebumps. No flutters. No thrill. No cock twitches. No feelings whatsoever. This is just getting so fucking confusing.

The bartender finally makes his way in my direction. I'm on my third *Jack* and *Coke*, and I really shouldn't have another, but I order one anyway.

When I put down my cash, Brandon sets his hand on top of mine. "I got it," he says, lightly nudging my money away from the bartender.

Oh, shit. He's hitting on me. What do I do?

He thought I was checking him out. I mean, I technically was.

"No, no, I got it..."

I try to intercept his hand, but the bartender grabs his money, giving me a wink. *Damn you, bartender. You just made this even harder.*

Brandon leans in my direction with a smile on his face, which I guess would be considered attractive to someone else.

"What's your name?" he asks in a husky voice.

"Liam. Um. Liam, but I think..." I don't even know what to say right now. "I'm not..." I add, trying to get out any string of words. "My friend," I say, pointing at Oscar across the room.

"Oh! Sorry. Gotcha. Misunderstanding. Sorry," he apologizes, holding up his hands.

Now he thinks Oscar's my boyfriend. Fucking great. If I were to ever have a boyfriend, it would not be anything close to Oscar. It would be like....well, Julian.

"Yep," I say under my breath, putting my head down and making my way back to our table.

When I look up, I see Oscar pointing at me. He's laughing so hard that he's clutching his stomach. This motherfucker.

"Dude! I saw that whole thing," he says, barely able to get his words out.

"Fuck off," I respond, taking a big gulp of my drink and sitting down.

"I'm dying! You just got hit on by a *dude*!"

"Yeah, so fucking what Oscar? You have something against being gay?" I say, slamming my hand on the table.

I'm actually really fucking offended by the way he's reacting. So what? Men can't hit on men now? What is this, 1950?

"Dude. Chill," Oscar retorts, sipping his beer. "Just funny is all," he adds, laughing under his breath.

"Yeah. Whatever," I grumble.

"What's your deal lately, bro? You've been irritable as hell."

"I'm not being irritable. You're just being a dickhead." I take a long pull of my drink.

I need to slow down. I don't need to be drunk while Oscar is pissing me off.

Just as I set down my glass, my phone goes off. I see the name *Jules* appear on the screen. I really need to change his name over to Julian.

JULES: Hey, I don't know if you're busy, but you said you'd help with Fishsticks if I ever needed it, and well, I could use an extra hand if you aren't busy.

I don't have to think twice. Fishsticks needs help? I'm there.

I'm on my way.

"Gotta head out," I say, gulping down the last of my drink.

"You're not driving, right? You've had three of those," he says, pointing to my now empty glass.

"Nope, walking," I grunt, pocketing my phone and grabbing my keys. "I'm not drunk anyway, just a little buzzed."

I head for the door and make my way over to Julian's apartment. He's three blocks down, and I power walk the whole way. I'm on a mission. To help him with Fishsticks. Yes, Fishsticks.

Yeah, that's it. This is about Fishsticks.

I quickly buzz Julian's apartment, hoping I remembered the right apartment number. I'm immediately let in. I make my way up the stairs, taking them slowly.

What the hell am I doing? Breathing in and out purposely to steady myself, I lightly knock on his door.

"Hey," he greets as he swings the door open.

He moves to the side, giving me room to walk through. I brush past him, and it happens again. That fucking feeling. The weird fluttering feeling that I didn't get from any other men at the bar tonight.

"So, Nora's out on a date, and I can't get Fishsticks to—"

Fishsticks comes up to my leg, nudging it with his head. I bend down to pet his back and look up at Julian. "Want me to hold him while you do your thing?" I ask.

"Yeah, that'll work," he says with an amazed look in his eyes. "He's just never like this with anyone. James was his person and—" He leaves off the end of his sentence with nothing but sadness in his voice.

"I'll help any way I can," I say.

And I will. I'd give him anything. All he has to do is ask.

I scoop Fishsticks up in my arms and take him to the couch. "Fishsticks, are you gonna be good and take your medicine?" I ask him in a sing-song voice.

Julian starts to make his way to me with a needle in his hand. I move my arms out of the way. I have no idea how this works. How do you give insulin to a cat?

"Hm. Yeah," Julian hems. "Okay, just hold him like that. *Real still.*"

"Just don't...poke me with that thing, please," I say, motioning to the needle with a grimace.

"*Real. Still,*" he repeats, instantly invading my space.

I take a deep breath, holding Fishsticks between my arms. I can feel Julian everywhere. He smells clean. Like soap mixed with a little bit of something manly. He's not wearing any cologne. It's just him, all Julian. Just his smell is turning me on. His arm brushes against mine as he reaches for Fishsticks' neck. Before I know it, he's gone, and it feels like something is actually *missing.*

I glance up. "Done?"

"Yep. All done. Thanks. For coming here so fast. I really appreciate it," he adds.

"Anything. Anything you need, I'm here," I say with a serious tone in my voice.

Wow. That came out a little...stronger than I meant it to.

"Yeah. Thanks. It means a lot," he says, still holding my stare.

I gently move Fishsticks off my lap and stand up. I've got to get out of here. "I should..." I say, pointing to the door.

"Yeah, for sure. Thanks again."

We make our way to the door. When I stop, I look into his eyes, searching for some type of feelings that may live in there.

Does he feel this? How can he *not* feel this? It's so overwhelming that it takes up the whole room. It feels like it takes up the whole fucking world.

Jules tilts his head to the side. "You okay?" he mutters.

He's asking me a question, but my thoughts aren't computing enough to answer him. My brain can't work properly when he's in my presence.

"Fuck it," I mutter, closing off the space between us. "I have to know," I add more to myself before crashing my mouth into his.

His lips are warm and soft beneath my own, and when his tongue swipes my lips, seeking entrance, I let him in willingly. Nothing could have prepared me for how this would really feel. I let out a long groan, and his tongue dives deeper, more frantically against mine.

This is exactly how I imagined it would be. It's explosive, like fire running through my veins. Pulling back, I look into his eyes, searching for answers he can't give me.

Did he just feel that too? Our chests heave together, our eyes holding secrets we're too scared to be let known.

I nod my head once, signaling to him that *yes*, we *should* do that again. He closes the space between us, taking my lips into his. This time it's gentle, like he's taking his time, wanting to savor every taste of me. When I hear him groan into my mouth, I capture it, breathing it into me. I want it to invade every part of me. I pull away slightly, pulling his bottom lip with me, giving it a gentle tug.

His hands come up and grip my hips, pulling me back to him. Demanding more of me. I feel his hard length between us, and instead of being scared, it is pure ecstasy knowing he feels this too.

Out of breath, I pull away. "Fuck," I mutter.

My whole body feels like it could explode. This is too much. I almost feel suffocated beneath it all. I need to breathe. To think. My body is in complete overload. I've never...felt *this* before, with *anyone*.

I murmur under my breath, "I....um...gotta go."

He stares at me, eyes hooded and full of lust. "Okay...."

Turning the knob, I look back. "Bye, Julian," I whisper under my breath.

Not waiting for a response, I shut the door behind me. The second I hear it click I know that I fucked up.

CHAPTER 25

The slam of the door jolts me straight out of my stupor. I blink slowly, my eyes adjusting to my surroundings and Liam is...he's...he's *fucking gone.*

The first man I've kissed since James and the guy just *leaves.* He walks out the door without a second glance.

I let my head hit the wall with a *thump*, catching my breath. My heart is racing, clanking around in my chest like it wants to jump straight out of my body.

I know that Liam says he's not gay, but straight men don't kiss men, and certainly not like *that.* I think that was the most intense kiss I've ever experienced in my life. It was pure unadulterated need, so full of desire that my legs almost collapsed beneath me. That was the kiss you see in Nora's rom-com movies, not one you get to experience in real life. But I just did, and it was other fucking *worldly.*

The fact that Liam has been feeling what I've been feeling these past weeks hits me like a freight train. Could being with Liam be a real possibility? I originally had shoved the thought from my head, not wanting to get attached to a straight man combined with the fear of moving on from James, but that was not a straight man's kiss. That was an I'm-attracted-as-hell-to you kiss, and I want more of them. It was *one kiss.* One kiss and I'm already falling for him.

I haven't kissed anyone...since James. Oh, James.

I put my hand over my mouth and let out a soft sigh. Just like the jerk off session, I didn't think of James once during that kiss. I don't know if that's a good thing or a bad thing. Is that normal? Nothing about grief is normal. Nothing about life after grief is normal.

I straighten my spine, my brain spinning uncontrollably, trying to put everything into perspective. Liam left me standing here after one of the best kisses of my life and frankly, I'm a little pissed off about it. I've never felt anything like that before. I never even kissed James like that. Our kisses became a habit, second nature, something I didn't really think about, but that kiss—that kiss is one I'll be thinking about for a long time.

Getting my bearings back, I stomp to my room on shaky legs. I'm mad, because really, that actually happened. I just got the best kiss of my life, and I was abandoned by the person who delivered it. As pissed off as I am, my cock doesn't seem to take notice of it. I adjust myself as I pull back my covers. It's me and my hand tonight. Same old, same old.

Just as I pull the covers over my head to try to ignore my semi, my phone dings with a notification. I want to ignore it, but Nora is still out on her date. I'd never be able to live with myself if she ended up in a ditch somewhere because I ignored her text message.

Yanking my covers down, I pick up my phone off the nightstand and find Liam's name on my screen. He messaged me. It better be an explanation.

LIAM: I'm sorry. I just needed to process that.

Wow. There is nothing more that I love than a man who admits when he fucks up. Which part is he sorry about though? That's the real question here.

ME: Sorry for what? The kiss? Or leaving after it?

LIAM: For leaving like that.

I want to celebrate, but this is a guy who had the balls to show up to our coffee date in person to let me know he thought I was a woman, when he could have just bailed on me. Is he just sorry for leaving because his chivalry tells him he should let me down in person rather than via text?

Wiping my sweaty palms on my comforter, I respond with pure honesty. Nothing like putting my already fragile heart on the line, right?

ME: So, not the kiss?

LIAM: Not the kiss.

He's not sorry for the kiss. My body instantly responds, my heart fluttering away in my rib cage.

ME: That kiss...was a lot.

LIAM: Yeah, sorry. I shouldn't have left like that. I should have explained.

ME: I get it. I had to think too. You're the first person I kissed since...

LIAM: You're right. I shouldn't have kissed you like that.

Crap. I don't want to scare him away by making him think I'm not ready. Funny how now that the moment comes when I have to make a choice about whether or not I'm ready, the answer is easier to give. If I was ever going to be ready to move on after James, it would be for a guy like Liam and kisses like that. Time to be a bold hunk of man meat, as Nora would say.

ME: Yes. You should have. How did that kiss make you feel? I need to know. I need to know what's going on in your head. Because for me, that was amazing.

LIAM: Yes. Amazing.

A breath of relief floods past my lips, followed by a smile. He's with me. Thank God he's with me because I need more of him. Before I can respond, another text comes through.

LIAM: My cock is hard just thinking about that fucking kiss.

Holy shit. This man.

ME: If you're planning on making a move, right now would be the time to just go for it.

Please, just go for it Liam.

LIAM: You want to know how hard my cock is, just thinking about you?

ME: Yes.

LIAM: Well, it's fucking throbbing.

LIAM: Fuck. That ass of yours is going to be in my dreams all night.

I can't believe this. Liam has been checking out my ass. *All. This. Time.* I swear, my cock is rock hard just knowing that he's been checking me out. I do have a great ass.

ME: That kiss made me want to do more than just kiss you...

LIAM: What would you do to me?

ME: Filthy things.

Oh, I could do dirty, *filthy* things. My imagination must have gotten the best of me because a ding interrupts my fantasies about all the obscene ways I could jump his bones.

LIAM: Use your words, Julian.

ME: I want to tear your clothes off your body.

LIAM: Are you touching that hard cock that I felt between us earlier?

Grabbing the lube off the nightstand, I slick up my hand.

ME: No, but I'm about to.

LIAM: Move your hand. Touch yourself and imagine it's me.

LIAM: Tell me all the things you'd do to me.

ME: I'd take your cock in my hands and make you come so hard you won't remember your name.

ME: I want to make you feel like no one has ever made you feel before.

Lazily, I move my hand up and down my shaft. I want to make this last as long as possible.

ME: Are you with me, Liam?

LIAM: I'm with you.

LIAM: Would you put me in your mouth?

ME: I'd run my tongue along your shaft while staring up at your lust-filled eyes. Every second you're in my mouth, I'd want to feel your cock get harder and harder for me.

ME: I'd take you so deep, you'd hit the back of my throat. Could you handle that?

I begin to stroke myself faster, thinking about what I would do to him. God, the things I want to do to him. The things I could show him. The way I could make him feel. Why hasn't he responded yet?

ME: I'm using my words, Liam.

I lift my head off the pillow, a loud noise interrupting my sex-filled thoughts. Nora must have finally made it home. I drop my head back down and focus, not wanting to be interrupted right now.

LIAM: Open the fucking door.

Open the…? Oh, fuuuck.
He's back?
Holy shit. He's here!
I yank the covers down and pull up my pants. When I open the door, I stop, waiting to see if he'll change his mind and leave or make his way up the stairs. His strides are rushed, taking two steps at a time.

When he finally makes it, I look at him for permission to make a move. He's squinting his eyes, assessing me. Before I can get any words out, he closes off the space and kisses me again. This time it's soft and slow, like he's exploring every single part of my mouth. The way his lips are melded into mine makes my body lose control all over again.

Yanking him through the door, I kick it closed behind me with my foot. I know he thinks he's straight, but I'm dying to show him how I can make him feel. I can rock his fucking world, if he just gives me the chance. Reaching down to his pants, I grip the outline of his cock in my hands, rubbing up and down. It's straining through his jeans, begging to be released. Just begging for me to take it in my hands.

Working my other hand down to his chest, I tug at the hem of his shirt. He releases my lips, swinging the shirt over his head and throwing it across the living room.

"Bedroom," I grunt.

I don't need Nora walking through the door, ruining my chance to show Liam how I can make him feel. I would never forgive her.

Grabbing him by his hand, I lead him to the bedroom, slamming the door shut behind me. Yes. This is really happening, and I want it to.

Standing back, I give him a heated stare. "Look at you," I murmur, admiring his lean chest, his strong arms.

I slowly make my way toward him and kiss his collarbone. I make my way down to his chest, taking his nipple in my mouth, giving it a gentle tug between my teeth, his chest rising and falling beneath me, obediently standing still to let me do whatever I want to him.

"Fuck, Julian fuck," he mutters, his eyes half-closed.

I can't get enough of my name on his lips. I want to hear it again. And again. And again. His hands are running through my hair, pulling it at the back of my neck. He tugs me up slightly, making me look up at him.

"Say it again. Say my name again."

"You...it's just you Julian," he whispers.

I'm not sure what that means, but I'll be sure to address it later. I'm too distracted by the sound of my name on his lips.

When I go back in for the other nipple, he grabs me by the back of my head, making me stay exactly where I am. I give it a long pull, making him grunt with pleasure.

"What are you doing to me?" he pants.

He takes my hand to his cock, making me feel how hard he is. "Do you feel this?" he asks.

"Yeah. Are you going to let me have it?" I ask, wanting permission to satisfy this uncontrollable need.

"Fuck yes. I've been dreaming about this, fantasizing about this," he responds, rutting into my hand, seeking more friction.

Going for his jeans, I start unbuttoning them. "I'm gonna make you feel so fucking good," I whisper while moving his pants down past his knees.

I go back up for another kiss, one that will make him lose his mind. I dive into his mouth with eagerness. My movements are frantic. Seeking him, wanting him with every ounce of my being.

Reaching down, I adjust my own cock through my jeans and decide to go for it. He's here. He's with me, and he's enjoying this. I want to make this good for him, and for me.

Pulling out my own length, I take it in my hands, joining it with his. "Together," I grunt between kisses.

I start working us both, Liam rutting into my hand, groaning against my mouth. I've never been so turned on by grunts before. I want all his fucking grunts. My hand starts moving faster and faster, taking us to the edge.

"Fuck. Fuck. I'm gonna...I'm gonna," he moans.

"Not yet. Wait for me," I demand, slowing my hand down.

I want us to go into this bliss together. I want to feel this at the exact moment he does.

Lifting my palm, I spit in it, trying to give us some type of lubrication. Liam looks at me with sex-fogged eyes, takes my hand away, and supplies his own saliva. Holy shit. He's going into this like a champ.

This time, I grab just him, his cock is pulsing in my hand. I move my hand down to his balls, warm and drawn up tight, rolling them around gently. I'm so determined to make this great for him.

He jerks his body back. "Keep that up and I'm not going to last another fucking second," he says, pushing his mouth against mine.

I can't get enough of the way he kisses me. It's explosive, all-consuming, like I'm the only thing that matters.

Taking us both, I mutter, "Come in my hand, Liam. Coat my cock with it."

He looks down, immediately spilling into my hand at my request and the sight of us together.

I'm just behind him, his warm release soaking my cock, making me come in long hot spurts while I continue to work us both. He grunts as he continues to spill, mixing us together.

When I look up, I find him still looking at our joined flesh, staring at us with hooded eyes. When he sees that I'm still coming, he grabs my ass with both hands, yanking me closer to him.   "That's it, baby," he whispers, pressing his lips and hot breath to my ear.

Hold up. Did he just call me *baby*? And did I just like it?

When I've come down from my climax, I look into his eyes for some kind of hint as to where he wants to go from here. What will he do now? Will he change his mind? Will he leave like last time? I can't keep doing this if he's going to leave every time.

He kisses me again, tugging my bottom lip with his teeth like he doesn't have a single regret about what just happened. He kisses me slowly, peppering his lips along my neck and chin.

"Do you, um, need help with Fishsticks...in the morning?" he asks with a hopeful smile.

"Fuck yes, I do," I answer without even thinking.

Thank God. There is nothing more I want right now than this man's lips back on mine and his body in my bed.

CHAPTER 26

Yawning, I stretch my legs out only to find another leg against mine, a manly, hairy leg. Looking over, I see Julian sprawled out on his back. His mouth is half open and he's completely naked. The white down feather blanket covers only his bottom half, his chest on full display.

My eyes take in his body, which is much like mine. He has a speckle of hair below his belly button. His arms are muscular, but smaller than mine. I look up to his face, his brown hair a mess with a single hair drooping over his forehead.

Reaching my hand out, I gently graze his chest with my finger, trying not to wake him just yet. I've never been attracted to a man. I've never had a magnetic pull to anyone like I have with him. Everything feels overwhelming when I'm in his presence, my senses heightened like seeing everything through a new set of eyes. The way he makes me feel is something I can't wrap my head around, but I do know that I don't want the feeling to go away.

And so fucking what if it's a man? If someone can make you feel like this, it doesn't matter. It should never matter. Feeling like this could never be wrong.

I move one finger to his jaw, to the place where I peppered kisses across just last night when we shucked the rest of our clothes and burrowed under his covers. Moving my thumb to his mouth, I shift the pad of my finger gently from side to side. Tracing his soft lips, feeling them under my touch makes my brain go haywire. These are the lips I kissed last night, multiple times, and I don't regret a second of it.

Lifting myself up on one arm, I watch his sleeping face, drinking him in. I don't know what the fuck this is, but nothing has ever felt this right. Leaning down, I kiss his cheek. He moves slightly, letting out a whimper. I give the side of his jaw a gentle suck, wanting to memorize his taste.

My eyes flicker up to his, seeing his halfway open now. His lip twitches, fighting off a smile.

"Good morning," I whisper.

"What? You ready to go again?" he says, stretching his arms above his head and yawning.

"I was just, well—" I stutter.

I don't know what I was doing. I've never woken up next to someone in the morning and wanted to stick around, wanting to feel their body against mine. It's completely new for me.

"You want me to go?" I ask, sitting up on my elbows.

Fuck, am I a one-night stand? Am I like one of those girls I run away from in the morning?

"Like hell I do," he says, grabbing me by the back of my neck and bringing my face to his. "Unless you want to go," he adds, sounding uncertain.

"No, I don't want to go," I say, melting into him.

I've never in my life not wanted to go. I go in for a kiss, wanting to feel that special feeling again. The feeling of being consumed by him.

"Let's brush our teeth first," he says, sitting up. "I have an extra toothbrush you can use," he adds.

"Thanks. Do we need to give Fishsticks his insulin?" I ask, knowing that was my excuse to stay here.

"Yeah. We'll grab him after a shower. You want to join me?" he asks, moving his eyebrows up and down suggestively.

"Sure," I answer nervously.

I've never showered with a man before, but then again, I've never done what I did last night with a man either. I'm not ready to have his body be much farther away from mine.

He starts grabbing his clothes from his dresser and putting them on while my eyes roam over his naked body. When they make their way down to his ass, my cock twitches. My body is clearly telling me it wants things that I'm not certain how to do. I start to distract myself, gathering my clothes from last night off the floor.

"Here's a shirt. I think yours is out there in the living room some-where," he says, throwing me a plain T-shirt from the dresser. "We're around the same size," he adds while looking me over. "So, me and Nora...we share a bathroom. Let's be quiet going down the hall. I don't like dealing with her until after I've had my coffee."

We tiptoe into the hallway, finding Nora's bedroom door still closed. I follow Julian's lead, sticking close behind him as we creep into the bath-room. He turns on the water, and I slowly begin to take off my clothes while watching him do the same. I catch him glancing at my cock, which is embarrassingly already at full attention. Fuck, just watching him un-dress has me about to lose my mind.

Giving me a wink, he steps into the shower, leaving the curtain partially open. With women, I'm usually the one making the advances, taking control. This switch of roles is so jarring, but it's fucking intoxi-cating. He's in charge and he knows it, and I'm going to hand over every ounce of trust to him.

Stepping into the shower, I find him with his back to me, water running through his hair. I watch the droplets in slow motion, following them with my eyes. They run down his sides, his arms, and his ass. I've never seen something so sensual in my life.

"Hey," I say, placing my hands around his hips.

I'm not fucking ashamed of this. I want all of him. The feeling when we are together is so intense, so strong. It's so undeniable that I don't think I could fight it if I wanted to.

He grabs my hands. "Should we...talk about this?" he asks apprehensively.

"Not right now," I whisper into his ear.

I don't want to talk right now. I pull his back into my front, letting him feel the reason I don't want to talk.

"Shit," he says under his breath while turning around to face me. He looks down at my cock, immediately dropping to his knees.

Pushing me against the shower wall, he kisses the inside of my thigh. "Can I?" he asks while looking up at me.

"You don't have to fucking ask. I trust you," I say, my voice husky, my heart nearly pounding out of my chest with anticipation.

"Turn around," he demands.

I look down at him quizzically. Turn around? I thought he was...

"If you trust me, turn around," he says again, his eyes gleaming.

I give a single nod and turn around. I brace myself against the wall of the shower and look over my shoulder.

"Like this?" I ask, unsure.

"Exactly like fucking that," he says, putting his hands on my ass.

"This ass is so sexy," he mutters, massaging my cheeks. "And I fucking want it," he adds, swiping his tongue up my crack in one long sweep.

"Whoa! Shit!" I scream, going up to my tiptoes.

"You like that?"

"It...I didn't not like it," I admit.

"Mm, then get your ass back here," he says, grabbing me by my hips and pulling me back toward his face.

He lashes his tongue across me again, his tongue slowly licking me, sending shocks straight up my spine.

"Uh. Okay, yeah, I fucking like it," I pant.

"Tell me how much you like it," he murmurs.

He dives back in, his tongue diving directly into my hole. I let out a strangled moan. I don't even think it was a moan. My voice box must not be working correctly with this pure ecstasy coursing through me.

"Fuck, whatever you're doing, don't fucking stop," I snarl.

This is new to me, but it's fucking glorious. I stick my ass out, chasing his tongue. I glance back, looking at this man in this most intimate moment. He's devouring me, pure pleasure coursing through his veins.

"I need...I need," I whisper mindlessly, grabbing my cock and giving it a long stroke.

"Nuh, uh," he grunts, batting my hand away and grabbing me, stroking me while his tongue continues to lap me up.

"Yes! Fuck. Oh, fuck. I'm going to come!" I yell, backing my ass into him while he jerks me with fervor.

"Come for me, Liam. I want to see you come all over this shower wall," he says into my crack.

His words send me over the edge. His tongue makes another circle around my hole, making me see stars.

"Yes!" I shriek, rutting my cock into his hand faster while his tongue chases my hole.

"Oh my God, Julian," I pant as my release coats the shower wall, my legs almost giving out.

I have to use effort to hold myself up with my arms, so I don't end up on the shower floor. I rest my forehead against the tiles as I come down from my climax, trying to catch my breath. When I'm halfway coherent, I turn around, looking at Julian with pure admiration.

I don't know what that was, but I'm going to learn how to do it for him. He's now standing under the water stroking himself lazily, a look of satisfaction in his eyes. His cock is so hard it looks painful. I've never touched his...shit. I've never done this before.

He looks at me, his eyes glassed over with desire. I know I need to do something. I can't leave him hanging, but I have no idea what I'm supposed to do right now. I have no idea what he likes.

"I don't..." I start, looking down at his hard cock. "I want to help... but, what...—"

Acknowledging my dilemma, he takes my hand and latches it around his cock. His hand is over mine, guiding my movements, making me less nervous. I watch with wonder. It feels like, well, like a cock. Like mine, but a little different. A little thicker, his tip redder than mine.

I continue following his lead, him teaching me how to make him feel good. I'm so turned on by him showing me how to do this to him that my cock is almost ready to go again. I drop to my knees, deciding my lust has mustered enough confidence to take this to the next level. He gave us a hand job last night. He took me in his mouth just now. He's had almost all of me. I want all of him too. I want to know how he tastes.

"I don't have a gag reflex." I smile up at him as he gapes down at me in surprise. "I don't know what I'm doing, but you can do what makes you feel good," I say, leaning back against the shower wall in invitation.

I stare at him, feeling like it's bursting from every cell in my body, my mouth open in welcome. I'm almost drooling from how turned on I am. Just being on my knees in front of him with my mouth open for his use has me fighting back the urge to come.

"Take control, Julian. Please," I add, just in case he's not sure if he should.

His eyes hood at my request. "You don't have a gag reflex?" He repeats back to me.

"No, I don't. Who knew all this time that it would come in handy?" I smirk, licking my lips and opening my mouth for him again.

He moves slowly toward me, his voice dropping an octave. "You want me to...fuck your face? Are you sure?"

"If I'm down here, it's because I want to be," I assure him, fisting my cock. "This is the place I want to be, understand?" I say sternly. "Now use me. I want to make you feel good."

Not asking again, he grabs his cock and glides it slowly in between my lips. I close my mouth around him gently. I've gotten plenty of blow jobs in my life, so I know what feels good to me. Does the same thing feel good to him?

"Tap my thigh if you want to stop," he tells me, putting his hands on the shower wall above me.

I nod my head in agreement while looking up at him, acknowledging what he just said with his cock in my mouth.

With a long, shuddery breath, his eyes never leaving mine, he rasps, "Now be good and suck."

I close my mouth tighter around him, my cock giving a violent twitch of arousal at my own obedience. If anything crossed the path of our gazes now, it would be incinerated. There's a carnal wave in the air, an unspoken acknowledgement that this magnetic behavior is unique to just the two of us. Something about the way he's looking at me with unbridled desire tells me he didn't ever say anything like that to his husband, and it makes me giddy inside knowing I can fulfill an unexplored need for him.

Slowly, he moves into my mouth, in and out, watching me from above. Memory tells me to use my tongue. I swirl it around his tip, tasting him, a pleasant saltiness that tastes like Julian smells, then I drag my tongue back down to his sensitive underside, knowing that's what I like.

He shudders above me, eyes rolling into the back of his head. It looks like I'm doing something right.

"Shit, that's it. Just like that," he whispers while thrusting his hips toward my face.

Taking me by the back of my head, he moves into my mouth even deeper. Yeah, not having a gag reflex is really fucking helpful right now. If I did, I'd have definitely thrown up all over his cock. He begins to move my head for me, making me take him exactly how he wants it. I reach around and grab his ass, pushing him farther down my throat, letting him know I can take even more of him. He hisses above me, eyes on me the whole time.

"My cock looks so fucking good in your mouth," he hums, while looking down at me, making me feel more confident. "Fuck yes, so fucking sexy," he grunts, while rubbing my cheek with his thumb.

I can feel him hitting the back of my throat while he grunts above me, using me and taking exactly what he needs. Just the way I told him to. It's never felt so good to give someone something.

"Yeah baby, take it. Take my cock. Take all of me," he repeats, moving faster and faster.

He called me *baby*, just how I slipped and called him *baby* last night. A feeling of warmth runs through my whole body. I love the way he praises me even though I'm clueless.

"Fuck," he pulls off me, panting above me. "I want to make this last as long as possible. Your mouth takes me so fucking well, like it was fucking made for me," he whispers, his chest heaving.

The mere fact that I'm having this effect on him turns me on. My balls draw up even higher at his words. My cock is getting harder and harder by the second.

"You ready, baby?" he asks.

There's that word again. That word that floods me with warmth.

"Keep calling me that, and I'll do whatever you want," I say, nodding my head at him while opening my mouth, ready for more.

When he slides in again, I swallow around him. He lets out a long moan above me. I'm learning by his sounds exactly what he likes. I never knew being on my knees for someone would make me feel this powerful.

Reaching down to my own cock, I stroke it slowly, trying to ease the need building up inside of me. I've never recovered from an orgasm so fast.

When he looks down and sees that I'm hard and ready again, he smiles. If we keep this up, I'm going to come twice.

"That's right. Stroke that cock for me. I want to see you come again."

My speed picks up with his permission, my hand moving frantically. Thank God. I may not have been able to hold this back.

He sends his hips back, removing himself from my mouth again. "I want to wait for you," he growls, holding my head in place.

I pick up my pace while he stares down at me. I've never jacked myself in front of anyone before. I didn't know how turned on I'd be from someone watching me. Or is it because it's Julian who is watching me?

"Are you gonna come for me soon, Liam?" he asks, his voice full of need.

I grunt, opening my mouth to let him know I'm almost there. He invades it again, this time not holding back. He moves his hips fast and hard while I try to use my tongue to hit the spots I know he likes.

"Fuck. Fuck yes. I'm going to come," he says between thrusts.

He suddenly pulls off me, taking his hand to his cock and jacking himself above me. I watch as he comes, moving my hand in sync with his. We both spill onto the shower floor, letting out long moans while staring into each other's eyes. It's the most intimate thing I've ever experienced. I watch him until he's empty, completely mesmerized.

When he's finished, he grabs my hand, helping me up. "Was that, was that okay?" I ask. "I mean, I've never...obviously."

"You were so fucking good," he says, putting his arms around my sides and pulling me closer to him.

"I wasn't...um...terrible at that?" I question, wanting to know the truth.

I want to make sure I can make him feel the same way I feel when he touches me. I want to be able to give him everything.

"You were fucking amazing," he says, grabbing my ass and pulling me into his naked chest.

"But the water is going to go cold soon," he says with a chuckle.

When we get out of the shower, he hands me a toothbrush. "It's new."

"Keep these things handy for your overnight guests?" I wink at him, knowing that I've done the exact same thing.

"Nah, Nora has a thing about toothbrushes," he says, pointing to a *Post-It note* on the mirror.

"You're blue, and she's green?" I ask, looking over at him as he brushes his teeth.

"The great toothbrush incident of 2022 has scarred her for life." He chuckles under his breath.

"Um. *The what?*" I ask, tilting my head.

"We were both the color green. Big mix up. I thought I was lime green. She thought she was lime green. You can see how that's a problem." He laughs, spitting in the sink.

I make my way across the counter, putting toothpaste on my toothbrush. "Never have the same color toothbrush. Got it."

I rinse my mouth out, putting the toothbrush on the counter when I see a group of pens scattered in the corner. Laughing, I pick up the pen adding, *Liam: Yellow* to her note. Julian looks at me in the reflection of the mirror, a smile on his face.

"Just to mess with her." I smirk.

I'm not trying to leave my mark like a clingy, um, boyfriend? Not boyfriend. Clingy friend? Yeah, *friend*, I guess? I don't know what this is, but I do know that friends don't do...what we just did in that shower.

JULES

CHAPTER 27

We make our way down the hall quietly, not ready to wake up Nora. When I reach my bedroom door, I find a *Post-It note* affixed to it. Well, safe to say that we woke her up. Damn.

YOU BETTER CLEAN UP YOUR FUCKING MESS!

The message is written in angry capital letters in typical Nora fashion. Good thing I already cleaned up my *fucking mess*.

I pull it off the door and walk into my room, dropping down in my office chair with a sigh. Holding it up for a second so that Liam can read the message before I toss it in the trash, I inform him, "She heard us."

He lets out a chuckle. "I guess I was louder than I thought I was, huh?"

"We both were. Now I'll never hear the end of it." I laugh.

At least I'm prepared for the third-degree I'm about to get from her. I'm sure she's ecstatic I got myself laid. She's probably in her bedroom giggling like a little schoolgirl.

Holy shit. I got myself *laid.* How come this is just hitting me? Sure, Nora is probably happy as a pig in shit, but am I? Did I just cheat on James? My husband is dead and I'm over here having sex with another man like it's not a big deal. This is a very *big deal.*

"I think we need to address the elephant in the room," I say, changing the subject.

I need to get straight to the point. I'm not going to avoid this conversation any longer. I refuse to get involved with a man who is going to keep me his dirty little secret. The way he high-tailed it out of here after he kissed me is telling me he's not ready for any type of real commitment. I'm thirty-six-years old and I've been married to another man for the love of God. I've been hiding in this apartment for the past year filled with grief. I'm done hiding.

"Yeah, I know, it's been a crazy twenty-four hours, huh?" he responds with a small sigh.

"So, turns out you're bisexual, huh?" I say bluntly.

"So, well, I don't think I'm bi..."

I let out a loud scoff. He can't be fucking serious. He just came for me...*twice.*

He looks up at me with a glare of disapproval. "Can I finish?"

"Okay. I'm listening...." I say, crossing my arms across my chest.

"It's just...*you* Julian. It's just you," he stutters.

I lean back in my chair, shocked by his admission. "Just me? How do you even know that?" I ask, leaning forward in my chair.

"Well, I tried to...ya know...to look at other men. This guy named Brandon was hitting on me at the bar the other night...and well...no one did what you do to me. I can't put into words what you do to me," he admits.

"Ha!" I let out a loud laugh. "Brandon from *Mixers*?" I ask with wide eyes. "He gave me his number that night you left the bar."

"Oh, I see," he says, looking at me with devastation, his eyes darting to the floor.

"I threw it away. I'm not looking for a meaningless fling right now," I add.

"So, that's not what this was for you then?" he asks me nervously.

"No. It wasn't. It's not."

I won't deny the pure electricity that courses through me when we touch, the way my chest feels like it could explode. I won't deny that when he kisses me, he completely consumes every part of me, or how I think of only him when we're together.

"Okay, but what about you? With James? How are you feeling about all of that?"

"I don't want to talk about me," I grunt out, turning my chair around and facing my desk.

"That's not fucking fair, Julian."

"You know what? You're right. It's not fair but mashing my feelings with your confusion isn't going to help this conversation." I swing around, looking him straight in the eyes.

He leans back, almost as if he's insulted. "*Confusion?* That's what you think this is? Me being *confused?*" he croaks.

"I honestly don't know, but what I do know is I'm not going to be used as an experiment for your sexuality. I've gone through enough. I can't stand the thought of that."

"Didn't I just show you how *not* confused I am?" he yells. "Fuck, look what just happened, what we just did! Wasn't it obvious that I enjoyed every damn second of it?"

"What am I supposed to believe, Liam? You tell me you're not gay, then you're sucking me off! Can you see how confusing this is for *me?*" I question, my voice raised louder than I'd like it to be.

"I don't know what this is, but what I do know is that it feels right. Everything feels right with you."

I gape at him, absolutely dumbfounded by his bold confession. I have no argument, because I know he's right. Whatever is going on between us feels *really fucking right.*

"It seems like you're just pushing me away because you're the one who's scared!" He accuses me when I can't find the words to respond. "It's fine if you're scared Julian, but don't take it out on me. Don't stop this because you're scared. I'm here for you. I promise I am."

He crosses his arms, waiting for my reaction. I still don't know what to say because he's right again. I am fucking scared. I'm scared of replacing James, but most of all, I'm scared of forgetting him.

His shoulders sag as the silence stretches and he purses his lips. "Call me when you're ready to admit it," he mutters, walking out the door, swinging it hard enough it slams shut behind him.

Digging my palms into my eyes, I let out a sob. I lay on my mattress, the only thing that's never let me down. Covering my head with my pillow, I try to hold the tears at bay. This past year, I've shed too many.

I fight them off, not wanting to let them win this time. Blinking them back, I force myself to swallow the sobs that are threatening to break free. I'm scared. I'll admit I'm scared, but will I let being scared take away any type of potential happiness that comes my way? Will I sit here and fight something I know feels right just because I'm fucking scared?

I haul myself out of bed, determined to somehow overcome this guilt and shame living inside my chest. Guilt for possibly moving on from James, and shame for pushing Liam away. He opened himself up to me, making himself completely vulnerable. He deserves the same from me.

Walking out of the living room, I find Nora sitting at the dining room table with a green smoothie and a scowl. Typical.

"Let's take care of Fishsticks," I say bluntly, not wanting to give her the chance to dig into me.

"Me and Liam already did it. Oh, and I gave him back his shirt. I found it on the floor this morning," she says, carrying her empty cup to the sink. "There's a cup of coffee left if you want it. Liam and I drank the rest."

"You and Liam besties now or something? Letting him drink your coffee and everything, huh?"

I'm being snarky as fuck, and I don't even care. I'm in a bad mood and she's going to give me hell, so I might as well be an asshole before she really lays into me.

"No. He just helped me with Fishsticks and had to deal with you. He deserved some kindness and a cup of coffee."

I scoff, "Yeah, whatever."

"I'm going to get in the shower, so I hope you cleaned it up," she says, pointing her finger at me.

"Yeah, I cleaned it up," I retort.

"You're a jerk, Jules. I hope you know that. These walls are paper thin, and I heard every word. I hope you know how wrong you just were."

I figured she heard it all. I mean, I can hear her hellacious singing while she's doing the dishes in my bedroom. I probably was a little harsh on Liam. I could have gone a little easier on him.

"What? You want me to be subjected to being someone's sexual experiment? You think that's really a good idea for me right now? You weren't here last night when he kissed me. You didn't see how he ran off all freaked out, and then he came back all hot and bothered. Hot and cold is the last thing I need right now. I need…stability," I babble, grasping for straws.

"Of course, he ran off. Straight or gay, lots of people run off when they first kiss someone. That's because it's scary for everyone to put themselves out there, you idiot. But he came back! The same night! That took balls, didn't it? So, don't try and use that whole sexual experiment bullshit as an excuse to push him away. You've been pushing everybody away for over a year because you're a coward."

Ouch.

Nora doing what she does best, putting me in my place with absolutely no filter. I know she means well, but damn. That was brutal.

I wince, pouring myself the last of the stale coffee. "Yeah, maybe I am protecting my heart, so what? Can you blame me? I'm not going to get another James," I counter, gripping the mug in my hand.

"If that's the case, he deserves better," she says under her breath.

Is she serious? How cold-hearted is that? I lost my freaking husband!

"Really? This from the woman who stood by my side at James' casket, crying with me," I choke up.

Shoulders sagging, she sighs. "No, Jules. I'm not minimizing the loss you feel from losing James, but I wouldn't be a good friend if I didn't try to kick your ass for making you see that Liam is clearly one of the good ones. The look on his face when he left…it was the kind when you try to give yourself to someone and they throw that gift back in your face. He doesn't deserve someone who's not going to give all of himself, so you shouldn't have given in last night if you weren't willing to give as much as he is."

Ouch again. This time, self-inflicted.

She's right. Liam does deserve better than me. He doesn't deserve to have to deal with my misery. I'm damaged goods. I don't think I can give all of myself right now, but the thought of Liam with someone else? Another man that isn't me? Rage courses though me. My brain can't make up its mind, but my heart knows exactly what it wants.

CHAPTER 28

I haven't heard from Julian for a week, and I won't lie to myself and say I've been fine. It's been anything but. In fact, it's been fucking excruciating. I've been waiting to have feelings like this for someone my whole damn life. When I finally get them, they're cut short before they even have the chance to grow into something life changing. I know that we could be life changing, if he'd only let us.

I don't care what he says, he's scared. He has every right to be. I know what grief can do to someone. He lost his husband, and I'm the first one who has come into his life since. He was sad and lonely, a shell of a man, but when we were together, I saw that spark in his eyes. His eyes give everything away, and deep down, I know he wants this. I wish he could see that I don't want him to stop loving James. I'm not asking him to stop loving him, I'm asking him to make room for me. I can never take James' place, and I don't want to. His grief over the death of his husband comes with him, and I would never try to take that away from him.

I can wait. I'll go slow. I'll do whatever he needs.

"Yo!" Oscar yells, waving his hand in front of my face.

"What?" I bark, yanking my earbuds out.

"What are you listening to?" he asks, tilting his head to the side.

"An audiobook," I snap out.

"Dude. You're listening to audiobooks and eating fruit. What the fuck is happening to you?"

"Maybe you should start eating fruit. You look like you've gained some weight," I say, gesturing to his stomach.

"Dude, really?" he asks, feeling for his abs that aren't there.

I shake my head. "What do you want? I'm working here," I say, pointing to the computer in front of me.

"Just making sure you got the event invitation in your email about the charity event. We're going together, right?"

"It's still a few weeks away. We'll figure it out." I sigh, shaking my head. "Now, go back to work, and stop finding reasons to bother me."

I pop my earbuds back in and hit *play*. Since I work in front of the computer all day, reading is the last thing I want to do when I get home at night, but I want to read Julian's books, so I got them on audio.

Damn. The man is talented. His words are like butter, melting into my brain.

Listening to these two guys being in love makes me wonder if this could ever be Julian and I. Walking hand in hand down the street. Kissing each other at a restaurant. Lying in bed and just cuddling. I'm so envious of these made-up people that it hurts. You'd think I'd be scared, scared of homophobia, coming out, telling my mom, all of it.

I'm not. The way Julian makes me feel when we were texting and when we're together makes all those things fall to the wayside.

I start typing in my long string of code for a website that I've been working on all week when I'm blindsided by the word *cock*. My fingers hover over the keyboard when I hear, *"take my cock into your hands,"* through my earbuds.

I'm transported to that night with Julian. That night he stroked us both into oblivion. That night when I realized I wanted all he would give me.

Shaking my head to try to remove the thoughts, I continue typing, when I hear something even more unexpected. One of the characters whispers into my ear, *"My ass. I want to feel you"*.

The words have me breaking out into a sweat, my cock rising in my pants. I yank at the first two buttons of my shirt, attempting to get some air. The character moans in my ear.

"I love the way you feel inside of me."

I'm completely immersed in these voices sharing this moment together. I imagine the voice as Julian instead of the man narrating. I imagine him, telling me how good my ass would feel for him, just like in his book.

Would it hurt? It sounds like it would hurt. I shift around in my chair, imagining how it would feel having a whole entire cock inside of me. I've had anal sex with women before, using lube and doing all the right things to make it comfortable for them. I know it can feel good for both parties involved. The women I've had it with seemed to enjoy it.

"Yes. Yes, baby. I need more."

Holy shit. This is the most intimate thing I've ever heard in my life. The way these two are pleasing each other this way. It scares the shit out of me, but I also realize with perfect clarity by the way my body's reacting that I want this with Julian. I want to give this to him. I want to give him everything there is to give of me.

I rip the earbuds out of my ears. I can't listen to another second of this. I'm at work, rocking a massive hard on and having fantasies about a man who cut me out of his life without a second thought. I rub my cock with the palm of my hand, adjusting myself beneath my pants. I really need another cup of coffee from the break room, but I can't leave this desk until my cock has calmed the fuck down.

Going back to the computer, I attempt to distract myself. As soon as I start typing, my phone dings from inside my desk drawer.

God. Please be Julian. Please. I say it like a prayer. Begging whatever God is up there to just help me out a little.

I close my eyes, squinting them shut before unlocking the screen. *Julian.* I look up to the ceiling, giving thanks that my prayer was answered.

JULIAN: Can we talk?

I type out a response as fast as I can. He has no idea that I've been sitting by this phone all week, waiting for him to text me.

ME: You want to meet?

JULIAN: First, I'm sorry it took me so long to text you.

ME: I understand. I'm glad you finally did.

JULIAN: Second, you're right. I am scared. You scare me, Liam. And what scared me most of all was how easily I let James' side of the bed be filled by you, but I want to try.

Before I have the chance to answer, my phone dings with another message.

JULIAN: Will you go out on a date with me? Like, a real date?

Did Julian...just ask me on a date? Like a date where two people hold hands and kiss in a restaurant, like an in-his-book-kind-of-date? My heart is ramming into my chest just thinking about doing what he describes in those books of his. I might be a little scared, but I know what I want, and I want this with every ounce of my being.

ME: Yes.

JULIAN: Tonight, 6? The little Italian place by the coffee shop?

ME: I'll be there.

My heart is thumping just thinking of this date. *Fuck.* I've never been so nervous in my life.

Julian wants to go on a date? *With me?*

I glance at the clock. Only two hours to go. Two hours until I get to go on a date with a man that will hopefully one day become *my* man. I mean, a boy can dream, right?

JULES

CHAPTER 29

I thought asking Liam on a date would scare him off, but he didn't even hesitate. By the mere seconds it took for him to respond, he didn't think twice. I know it was wrong of me to do it, but I wanted to test him. I need to know where he's at before getting myself involved with him. If he wants to hole me up in a closet and keep me a secret, I just can't do it. I'm not making room in my heart for someone besides James if they're not willing to make room for me in broad daylight. I can't put my already broken heart on the line for someone who could smash it to bits by not admitting to anyone else how he feels about me. A hook up is one thing, but what I feel when I'm with Liam is so much more than that. I'd want the real deal from him, anything less would be too painful to pretend about.

Walking out to the dining room, I find Nora on her laptop. "Hey," I say quietly.

I know she's still pissed at me. We've barely talked this past week. She's been avoiding me like the plague, and I can't say I blame her.

"What?" she asks, not even glancing up from her laptop.

Shit. She's madder than I thought. I have to fix this. Nora mad at me is a very unpleasant experience.

I sit across from her at the dining room table. "Listen, can we just talk?"

"Yep. Sure," she says haughtily, closing her laptop.

I put my head in my hands, looking down at the wooden tabletop. "I know I fucked up, and I'm going to try to fix it."

"Jules," she says, putting her hands down on the table, "James would want you to be happy. Please quit pushing away any little thing that could make that a possibility."

"I know, but…it's so fucking hard," is all I can get out before a single tear springs from my eye, running down my cheek.

"On the other hand, I'm happy you finally got some booty," she adds, making me bark out a laugh. "I heard you two in that shower and *holy hell, Jules.*"

"Yeah, it was pretty amazing. *He's* pretty amazing."

Giving me a stern look, she whispers, "Then don't fuck this up."

"What if he runs away? What if he can't deal with having feelings for a man? You know how much that would break me? I'm already broken, Nora."

Slamming her hands on the table, her voice goes up a notch. "You are not broken, Jules! I never want to hear you say that again. Do you understand? *You. Are. Not. Broken.*"

I nod my head back and forth, sighing. "But I feel broken."

"You've gone through a lot this past year, more than most of us go through in a lifetime, but you aren't broken. You're healing. There's a difference."

It hits me like an epiphany. She's right. I'm not a broken man. I'm a *healing* man, and I deserve happiness just like everyone else. I can't keep standing in my own way.

"I asked him on a date tonight," I say, lifting my head up to see her response.

"I also have a date tonight," she replies with a wink. "I'll be sure to go to her place afterward, so we don't have to hear you two making up," she adds, rolling her eyes.

"We weren't *that* loud."

THE RIGHT WRONG NUMBER

"Oh, God Juliannn," she imitates, throwing her head back.

"Don't tell me my business, devil woman!" I shout, getting up from my chair with a smile.

I'll admit it. We were really fucking loud. If this date goes well, hopefully we can be that loud again.

CHAPTER 30

I lean against the brick wall of *Marios,* the only Italian restaurant in town. It's considered fine dining, where the owner is actually Italian, not like those knock-off chain places that are everywhere.

I'm wearing some nice black slacks that I usually wear to work and my signature rolled up business shirt. Except this time, I rolled my sleeves up a little higher, knowing how Julian likes my tattoo. I tuck in the bottom of my shirt, making myself a little more presentable.

I've never been this nervous for a date. I've seen him buck ass naked, we made each other come multiple times, but my heart is still pounding in my chest. This is official now. It's a date. We're going on an actual date, and I don't want to mess it up.

When I see Julian walking down the street, I lift myself off the building to get a look at him. He's dressed up in blue business pants and a white short-sleeved button-down shirt. My body moves of its own accord. It attracts to him like a magnet. I take a few steps toward him and stop, watching him nervously run his hands through his hair. Those hands pulled at my hair while we were in the shower. Just the mental image has my cock twitching in my pants. Fuck. I'll never make it through dinner if I keep thinking about how great we are together. I shake my head, trying to clear the images of me on my knees for him.

"Um, hey," he greets me with a crooked smile. "I made a reservation."

"I feel so special. I'm reservation material," I chide, turning to open the door for him.

We sit at a small table in the corner. The dim lighting and quiet atmosphere are calming, loosening me up a bit.

"Thanks for coming," he says nervously. "I didn't know if you would."

"Why wouldn't I?"

"Well, the whole...um, being seen with me out in public thing. Didn't know if you were ready for it."

"Is this about the bisexual stuff again?" I ask.

I thought we had gotten past this. I don't care if I'm labeled bisexual or gay or whatever else. It doesn't matter when I feel like this. Label the fuck away.

He puts his hands on the table, his expression growing serious. I guess we're getting down to business.

"Listen, Liam. I'm a gay man. I've been married to another gay man. It's just that I need to know where your head is before going any farther, okay? If I'm going to allow someone into my life, I need to make sure it's someone who will help me live again, not hide. I've done enough hiding for a lifetime," he says, wincing and looking down at his hands.

I lean toward him, grabbing his tensed-up fist on the table and pulling it toward me. "I'm not scared of this Julian. Why would I want to hide something that feels like...*this?*"

His widened gaze darts to mine, then down to our hands that are now woven together, our fingers intertwined. "So, you're not freaking out?"

I squeeze his hand tightly. "No, because for reasons I can't explain, being with you feels right. How can I freak out when it feels like this is the place that I should absolutely be, with the person I should absolutely be with?"

I'm still holding his hand across the table when the waitress brings our drinks and takes our order. I don't let go the whole time. I squeeze his hand again gently, letting him know I'm all in. When she leaves, he pulls his hand away.

"Alright, I get it. Okay. Let's just...let's just take it slow. We've both had our worlds turned upside down in completely different ways. So, slow, okay?"

I lift my hands up in a show of surrender, trying to fight my smile of relief. "Slow is perfect. I'm good with slow."

When our food comes, I let out a grimace because I don't want this date to end. I haven't seen him in over a week. I'd spend all night with him in this dim little restaurant if we could.

"Tell me something about James. How did you two meet?" I ask, digging my fork into my spaghetti.

"You really want to hear about that stuff?" he questions me, his eyebrows raised.

"Yes. I want to know everything about you, which means I want to know about James too. I want to know all about the person who will always hold a piece of your heart."

He sits back in his chair, a stunned look on his face. "Um. Well, okay. Believe it or not, we met through Nora." He laughs, cutting into his eggplant.

"And?" I nod my head, hinting at him to continue.

"Well, James took some classes with Nora in college. She brought him home to study one night, and the rest is history," he says, waving his fork in the air.

"Oh, so you three were all friends?"

"Yeah. Nora moved out when me and James got serious. She moved back in after he died to help me out. I didn't handle it very well, obviously."

"How does she feel about you seeing someone?"

I need to know the answer to this question. Nora is a hard ass and his best friend. If she's not in, I don't stand a chance.

He looks up with that dreamy smile. "She likes you," he says, looking back down at his food and digging his fork into his eggplant parmesan. "Don't tell Mario this, but my mom's eggplant parmesan is way better than this," he adds, but that little smile stays on his face, telling me it's because of me having Nora's approval. Thank God.

"Got any good eggplant jokes?"

"Only inappropriate ones," he answers, smirking.

After we pay the bill, we walk out of the restaurant and stand on the sidewalk, both of us clearly not wanting this date to end. We stare at each other, each of us with questions in our eyes.

"So, um, Nora is on a date tonight, and, uh, Fishsticks needs his second dose of insulin. And, well, you know how he is..." he trails off, stuffing his hands into his pockets.

"Let's go," I say without a second thought, grabbing his hand from his pocket, goosebumps running up my arms.

I look in his direction, watching him glance down at our intertwined hands with a smile. I love that the sight of us makes him smile.

Yeah, Julian. I promise I don't give a fuck who sees us.

When we make it to his apartment, Fishsticks greets me in the doorway. I pull him into my arms, and he says *hello* with a loud purr. I take him to the couch and sit down to wait for Julian. I don't want to hold all twenty-five pounds of him for an extended period of time.

"Hey buddy!" I coo as Fishsticks *boops* his face against my chin. "I don't know why they talk so bad about you. I think you're a wonderful cat," I whisper, eyeing Julian with a smirk.

I watch as he prepares an insulin shot and approaches us slowly. "Alright Fishsticks, don't be an asshole," he pleads.

"Don't listen to him," I reassure the cat. "You're not an asshole."

Julian pulls at the scruff behind Fishsticks' neck and inserts the needle without any retribution. "I can't believe how much he likes you," he muses, "but I can't say I blame him. I kinda like you too," he whispers, bending down and kissing my cheek. "I've wanted to kiss that dimple since the moment I saw you," he groans into my ear.

"Kiss it all you want," I respond, moving my head, and kissing him on the lips.

Fuck. I want to give him everything, and I want everything from him. I shoo Fishsticks off my lap, moving him over to the couch cushion next to me. He scoots next to my leg, trying to get as close as he can to me. I give him a long stroke down his back while Julian discards the needle and makes his way back to me.

He pulls me up off the couch by my hand, slamming my body into his, chest to chest. My breathing goes erratic. It's hard to be this close to him and breathe normally, the way his eyes devour me, the way the energy in the room shifts to pure desire.

Leaning in, he kisses me slowly, our tongues seeking each other, demanding to connect. I open my mouth slightly, letting his tongue swipe against mine. When he pulls away, he takes my bottom lip with him playfully for a moment.

"God, what are you doing to me?" he groans, grabbing my hand.

He leads me into his bedroom, closing the door behind him. Walking toward me slowly, he walks me backward until the back of my knees hit the bed. Giving me one last gentle push, he knocks me flat on my back and crawls on top of me. He straddles me, his legs tight around my own. I let out a sigh. Having someone on top of me has never felt so right, so fucking perfect.

He runs his hands down my sides, up my arms, and back down again, sending goosebumps all over my body. Reaching for my buttons, he starts to undo my shirt slowly. I reach up, reciprocating. Once I finally get to the bottom, I rip his shirt off him in one pull.

"Fuck. You feel so good on top of me. Like you belong there," I rasp, digging my nails into his thighs.

I make my way to his waist, unbuttoning his pants. "Off," I demand.

He lifts off me, tugging his pants free while I do the same to mine.

"What do you want, Liam? Tell me what you want," he demands, leaning down and taking my nipple into his mouth, giving it a gentle bite then soothing it with his tongue.

I arch into him, rubbing my cock against his. "*You*," I breathe, my heart jackhammering in my chest.

"I'm so glad Nora is gone. I'm going to make you come so hard that you won't want to move for a week," he mutters under his breath. "You want to try something new?" he asks, his voice husky. "Do you trust me?"

"I don't know what I'm doing, but I'll try anything for you," I confess desperately.

I trust him with every ounce of my being. I'll do whatever he asks.

"On all fours," he orders while lifting off me.

I don't think twice as I flip over, getting on my hands and knees. I push my head into the pillow when I hear the nightstand drawer open and close. I shift my head to the right, noticing a bottle of lube in his hands.

I have my ass up in the air, on full display for him, but I'm not un-comfortable in the slightest. I'm neither ashamed nor insecure. I mean, he had his mouth there. He devoured it like he loved it, and finding out how good it feels to have him there makes me want to stick my ass in the air all day for him. I shift onto my forearms, looking back at him admiring me.

Taking his hand, he smooths it down my spine, making me arch higher and push back against the heat of his groin and thighs. He's hard and ready, so I push my ass tighter against him, wanting to feel his cock, wanting to feel every part of him.

"Nuh, uh," he grunts while bending his head down, his tongue diving straight toward me.

He laps at me just like he did in the shower. Fucking devouring me.

My ass pushes back into his face, wanting more. His tongue goes straight for my hole, making me gasp in pleasure.

"You're so good at that," I say into the pillow. "I can't wait for you to teach me how to do it."

His tongue swirls around my circumference, making me tremble. I can barely hold myself up.

Pulling back suddenly, he smacks his lips together "Why do you taste...minty?"

"Oh, I. Um, well, I used mouthwash. You know. Down there."

"You washed your asshole with mouthwash?"

"Yeah. I thought...well, I thought it would. I don't know. Taste better?"

"Oh my God. You're insane, and I love it," he says, cracking up. Leaning back in, he gives my crease one long tortuous lick.

"You still trust me?" he asks, looking in my direction for confirmation.

"Yes," I gasp out, barely a whisper.

"Ready?" he asks.

I nod slowly, putting my head back down onto the pillow.

I feel a finger circle me, making me whimper. It slides into me slowly, so fucking slowly, making me groan. I'm not exactly sure if I like it, but I'm not giving up yet. I'll try anything for him.

"Relax, Liam. I'm going to make this feel so good for you. I promise."

My body instantly calms at his words, my muscles turning to jelly. It's like even my muscles trust him.

He pours more lube down my crack, working his finger in just a little bit more. It burns, stinging slightly. When he gets past his first knuckle, I let out a small cry. I don't know what that was, but I do know I fucking liked it.

"Look at you, taking this so good," he says, pushing deeper inside me.

"Oh fuck," I groan, pushing my ass into him, making him give me more.

His finger goes deeper, searching for something. When he's found what he's looking for, I almost fly off the bed, stars dancing beneath my eyelids.

"Holy shit!" I scream, backing my ass up into him when he adds another finger, his fingers finding that spot again.

I let out a husky moan while rutting my ass into his hand. "Fuck, fuck, Julian. Fuck."

Jesus. I'm a broken record, unable to form proper syllables.

"That's it, baby. You're doing so good for me," he says as he adds another finger.

He's stretching me while hitting that spot that makes me go wild. My ass is wiggling in the air, seeking more. How have I been missing out on this all this time?

"So full," I whimper, grabbing my cock and stroking, trying to get some relief. "I need to come," I beg. "Please."

He reaches around me, taking my cock out of my hand and replacing it with his. He works both ends while I grip the bars on the headboard. Dipping his fingers in and out of me, he works my cock in tandem.

"Be good and come for me," he whispers while thrusting his fingers in and out, hitting that spot every time. "Paint my bed with it," he demands.

I let out a strangled cry. I can't take it anymore. The sensations combined with what his sultry commands do to me—it's too much. I'm an incoherent blubbering mess.

"God Julian. Oh my God," I scream, slamming my ass onto his fingers while his hand chases my cock.

"Yes, yes Juliannn," I cry out, coming all over the bed.

All over the sheets. All over the headboard. I come so hard I lose my vision. I'm gasping for air, shaking.

"Holy shit," I mewl uncontrollably.

I drop down onto the mattress that's filled with my release, unable to hold myself up any longer. When I hear Julian above me, working his lubed-up cock, I flip over, wanting to see him. Wanting to watch him when he comes. I swear it's my favorite thing to watch these days.

"On me. Come *on me*," I demand.

"You'd like that, huh?" he says while working his cock faster and faster. "Mark you as mine? Is that what you want?" he asks, looking down at me with hooded eyes.

"Yesss," I rasp as his release coats my stomach in long hot spurts.

He keeps working himself, his head tilting back while closing his eyes. He's shuddering above me, losing himself in his orgasm, and it's fucking breathtaking.

He drops on top of me, panting. His arms cage me in. I've got come all over my body. My stomach and back are sticky with us, and I'm not bothered by the mess. I take his mouth for a kiss. He unravels me at the seams, and I want more of this, more of him.

He lifts off of me, parting our connection, looking down at my stomach that's filled with him.

"Let's shower," he says, raising his eyebrows.

I leap off the bed. I swear I've never moved so fast. I know exactly what happens in that shower, and I love it.

JULES

CHAPTER 31

Opening one eye, I let out a yawn. Liam is in front of me, his arm over my shoulder. My arm is tucked under his body, my leg tangled up in his like a pretzel. I love the way this feels, the way we fit together.

Smiling to myself, I think about last night. Our date, holding hands at the restaurant, and the mind-blowing sex. The trust Liam hands over to me is intoxicating. He's all in, and I crave it. I crave him in a way I never thought I would crave anyone again. The way he just so easily conformed to this, to us, amazes me. I've only known him for two months, but he feels like he belongs here, like he belongs with me.

I'm falling for this man. When we're together, nothing else matters. There is no sorrow, no reoccurring memories of James looping through my mind like a movie. It's just me and him. Does feeling like this with Liam make James cease to exist? My mind battles so many of these questions, unsure of the right answers.

Reaching over, I swipe a finger along his jaw, watching his sleeping face. I could get lost in him. His strong jaw, his dirty blonde hair. The scatter of whiskers on the face. His vulnerability. The way he trusts so easily. The size of his heart. I'm consumed by every part of him. It feels like a dam breaking, and I'm no longer able to hold back the tide. I can't stop it, and I don't think I want to.

His eyes pop open, a smile breaks through his lips. I lean in for a small kiss. "Why did the tomato blush?" I mutter, smiling into him.

He kisses me back, rising above me. He moans repeatedly into my mouth, and I swallow them all down, breathing him into me. The way this man kisses me takes my fucking breath away. Like I'm all that matters, like I'm fucking everything.

"Why?" he lets out.

"Because he saw the salad dressing," I say, chuckling under my breath.

"Julian….do you feel this?" he asks, his hands coming to my shoulders.

"Yeah, I feel that," I answer, feeling his hard cock between us.

"Not that. This," he says, putting his hand flat on my chest.

"Yeah...I feel that too."

"What's happening to us?"

"I don't know, but I'm done fighting it," I whisper, pulling him into me by the back of his neck.

I take his mouth, devouring him. I can't get enough. It's almost like I would die if I didn't have him. He pulls himself up, sitting on top of me. His weight makes me sigh. Everything about being with him feels so complete. How can this feel so perfect? It didn't even feel like this with James. Nothing has ever felt like this.

Kissing down my chest he asks, "Can you teach me that thing you do? I want to make you feel like you make me feel."

"You already make me feel like you feel," I admit, taking his hand into mine and squeezing it.

He kisses his way down farther, making his way to my hard cock and kissing it. "This is mine," he says, taking the tip into his mouth.

"Yes, it's yours. Take it," I sigh, pushing my hips up to have him take me deeper.

He takes me in his mouth all the way to the base of my shaft. *Fuck.* I love that he doesn't have a gag reflex. I swear I'm the luckiest man in the world.

He continues sucking, licking, taking all of me until I'm a crumbling moaning mess. Just when I'm about to come, he stops.

"On your stomach," he demands, and I am more than happy to oblige. I slowly make my way to my hands and knees.

"You're so fucking sexy, every single part of you," he whispers, bringing his hands to my ass and massaging my cheeks gently, taking his time with me.

"Wow," he mutters.

"What? Is something wrong with my ass? It looks like yours, you know."

"Nope," he simply says, swiping his tongue up my crack. "Like that?" he asks, settling back on his feet.

"More," I grunt at him. "Yes. More. Just like that."

He swoops back in, eating and sucking me like he's starved for my body until I'm gasping and shuddering. He works his tongue around my hole, swirling against me. He makes his way to my balls. When he licks their underside, I shudder with pleasure.

"I need...I need," I stammer.

I can't take it anymore. My body feels like it's on fire, ready to explode.

He pushes my ass back, removing his mouth. "On me again, I'm yours?" he asks, a hitch in his voice as he rolls over.

"Fuck yes, you're mine. You're all fucking mine. You hear me?" I say, bringing him in for a kiss.

I situate myself above him, my hand moving at lightning speed. "Mine," I whisper with each stroke until I'm coming onto his stomach in thick hot ropes. I watch him looking up at me like the way he'd look up at the stars.

Leaning over, I take his mouth. "Mine," I say against his lips. I kiss his cheek. "Mine." I kiss his neck. "Mine." I work my way around his face, marking every single bit of it as mine. "I may be scared, but I'm not scared enough to let you go."

He breaks eye contact, turning his head to the side. "Do you smell that? Is that bacon?" he asks, my release still all over his chest and stomach.

I lift my head up, smelling the air. "Nora doesn't cook ba—*fuck!*" I rip myself away from him, throwing a box of tissues at him. "Clean up!"

"What? What?" he yells, glancing around in a panic.

"Brunch. My mom. I forgot!" I rant, digging through my dresser for a pair of jeans.

"Are you going to sneak me out of here like we're teenagers?" he asks, shoving his feet into his pants.

"Well, no. For one, that's not possible, we're on the third floor. And two, well, we're adults. It's just that my mom...well, she's..."

"I would love to meet your mom," he says as he grabs me by the shoulders, slowing me down. "But are *you* ready for me to meet your mom is the better question?" He looks at me, determination in his eyes. "It's okay if you aren't. I can stay in here until the coast is clear."

"Yeah, I mean, no. You don't have to hide out. You promised you wouldn't hide me, so I'm not going to hide you."

"Okay," he says, nodding.

"Are *you* sure you're okay with meeting her?" I ask.

"I'm totally okay with it."

"Okay. I'm just warning you, she's a little much."

"I got this Julian," he responds, yanking his shirt over his head. "It'll be fine. I promise."

We walk out into the living room hand in hand, giving no illusion about what is going on between us.

My mom turns around from her pan of popping bacon with a gasp. "Julian!" she screeches. "Who...who is this?" she asks us, pure happiness on her face.

"Mom, this is Liam. Liam, this is my mom," I introduce them, waving my hand between them.

"Hi, Julian's mom," Liam says, taking her hand and giving it a light shake.

"Diana. My name is Diana," she gushes. "Sit, sit, sit," she squeals, ushering us to the dining room table to join Nora.

"Hey, Nora," Liam says, bumping his shoulder against hers.

"Hey, Liam," she responds, a mischievous smile on her face.

"How long has she been here?" I whisper.

"We heard it all," she whispers back, chuckling.

Fuck, I mouth to Liam while she cackles beside me.

My mom sets a plate of bacon in front of us along with a plate of scrambled eggs. She sits directly across from me, her cheeks bright red, a huge smile on her face. I can already see it in her eyes, she's going to embarrass the shit out of me.

"Hey, Fishsticks. How ya doing buddy?" Liam asks, looking down as Fishsticks winds through the legs of his chair. "Did he get his insulin yet?" he asks, glancing over at Nora.

"Yep. I creeped up on him while he was asleep. I didn't want to interrupt, well, *all that*," she says with a laugh, motioning toward my bedroom door.

"Liam! It's so nice to meet you!" Mom interrupts. "Are you and Julian together? You two sure sounded like you're together a few minutes ago," she asks giddily.

Damn mom. Could you be any less subtle?

I put my head in my hands. "Yeah, Mom. We're together. We're taking it slow, so don't freak out," I add, scooping scrambled eggs onto my plate.

"Well, that's just wonderful!" she exclaims, clapping her hands. "I'm so happy for the both of you!" she adds. "So, hun, has this given you inspiration? You know, for those books of yours? I know you've had such a hard time," she laments, taking a bite of her bacon.

"No, Mom! I write fiction. I don't write about my real life," I huff.

She thinks just because I'm finally getting laid that I'm suddenly able to write? That's not how this works.

"He's an amazing writer," Liam adds, looking over at my mom.

"You've read my books?" I ask, completely dumbfounded.

Leaning back in my chair, I stare at him with pure admiration. He's read my books. My heart instantly fills up with something, I'm not sure what it is, but it feels good. Liam never ceases to amaze me. James only read the first one.

"Well, um, no. Not exactly. Because of my work, it's hard for me to read after staring at the computer all day. So, I listened to them instead," he states, taking a drink of his orange juice.

"*Listened* to them?" my mom asks.

"Yeah. I found an app for it on my phone," he answers with a shrug.

"Oh, that's amazing! All the things they can do these days with these phones! What's the app? I have trouble myself, especially if the font is small. My eyes aren't what they used to be," she says, pointing at her eyes. "I had to get those dreadful readers."

"Oh, I forget the name. Let me check," Liam says, pulling his phone out of his pocket and handing it over to my mom.

"Oh, it's in this entertainment folder? This one? *X-Videos*?" she questions, tapping the screen.

THE RIGHT WRONG NUMBER

"No! Not that one! No! Don't open..." Liam rushes out, trying to take the phone out of her hands before the app opens and sex sounds start playing through it.

I hear a snort from Nora. She's covering her mouth, trying to contain her laughter. Damnit. Why does she have to make this worse than it already is?

"That's...I was..." Liam stammers, his face red.

I can't hold it back any longer. I bark out a laugh. Tears start streaming down my face, my laughter in full force now. I'm completely hysterical, and I can't make it stop. I bend over in my chair, trying to catch my breath.

"I'll check out this *X-Videos* app! See if I can find any good books to listen to!" Mom says excitedly.

"No, no, no, Mom! Try *Audible*. That one's better for audiobooks, right Liam?"

I can't be the one to tell her that *X-Videos* is porn, not audio books. I refuse to talk to my mother about porn.

Nora suddenly gets up from her chair, trying so hard not to laugh that she's snorting. Her face contorts underneath her hand, unable to hold back any longer.

"I can't...I can't," she mumbles as she makes her way to her room, closing the door behind her.

Her door may be closed, but her laughter seeps out into the kitchen. She's lost it.

"I'd better get going. I have some work to catch up on. Thanks for the breakfast," Liam blurts. "It was great to meet you, Diana," he adds, pushing back his chair and standing to leave.

"Lovely to meet you too Liam! Come over for dinner this week so we can talk more!" she calls out.

Standing up, I follow him to the door. Bringing him in for a hug, he breathes into my ear, "I'm so sorry."

Laughing into his chest, I let out a giggle. "It's all good. I'll text you later."

Walking back to the kitchen, I join my mom to help her with the dishes. "I'll wash, you dry," I say, nudging her to the side and handing her a towel.

"I really like him, Julian," she says, taking a plate from me. "And he's nice to look at too," she adds, giving me a wink.

"Yeah, I like him too. *A lot,*" I sigh, James peeking back into my brain.

"Julian, moving on is hard. It will never be easy, but you have the strength and courage to move forward. I know you can do it," she says, bumping my shoulder with hers.

"I just…feel so guilty. Like I'm leaving James behind or something. Like I'm forgetting about him," I admit.

"Guilt is probably the most painful part of death," she says, dropping the plate in the dish rack, "but remember, those we love never truly leave us. There are some things that even death can't touch. He's here, and he's happy for you."

I let the next plate fall back into the sink. Still soapy and wet, I put my hand across her back, bringing her in for a hug.

"Thank you, Mom," I say, leaning my head on her shoulder.

She's right. It's time to let myself be happy, and Liam makes me happy. I've never been with someone who makes me feel like this, and in order to have it, I need to start treating it how it is, which is amazing. I'm done being my own worst enemy.

LIAM

CHAPTER 32

JULES: My mom wants you to come to dinner tonight.

ME: Are we sure that's a good idea?

I type, shaking my head. We already tried this once, and it was a nightmare.

JULES: It'll be fine, just no more porn please. LOL.

ME: OMG. I forgot I downloaded that to my phone.

JULES: It was hilarious. I'm still laughing about it. Be here at 6?

ME: I'll be there.

The first time I meet Julian's mother, I show her a freaking porno app. At least I caught it before the sex sounds started playing. In my defense, I only downloaded that app so I could watch gay porn to figure out what the hell was going on with me. I should probably tell him that to clear the whole porn thing up.

Shaking my head, I shuffle through my paperwork to figure out which project is next to work on when Oscar strolls into my office. I swear he can't go a single day without bothering me. He clings to me like freaking cellophane.

"Hey bro, bar tonight?" he asks as he walks through the door.

"Nope. I have plans," I respond.

"You got a date or something? You're always blowing me off lately. What's going on?"

"Yep, a date," I answer, looking down at my stack of papers.

"You're actually still talking to that Jules girl?" he asks.

I don't even know how to answer that. I'm not ashamed of me and Julian being together, but Oscar is a piece of work. If I tell him, I'll never hear the end of it.

Shit. I honestly don't know how he'll react after that scene he made in the bar when I got hit on by another man, and I really don't want to find out the answer to that while I'm at work.

"Yeah, with Jules," I mutter. "We'll hit up the bar next week," I add, trying to get him off my back.

I don't want to answer a million questions about *'Jules'* right now. The reaction at the bar that night was enough to let me know his reaction will not likely be the one I want to hear. I'm at work right now. I can't be going around punching people. I need this job.

"Alright man, but you can't back out. I need you. You're my wingman."

As soon as he walks out, I pop my earbuds back in and continue my audiobook while sorting through these never-ending files. I'm attempting to read all of Julian's books, but it's going to take a while. Turns out he's popular. He's got seven books in total, and his reviewers are demanding more.

I really do like his books, but I can't figure out why I'm not turned on during the sex scenes unless I'm imagining Julian and I together. I know Julian thinks I'm bisexual, but I just don't think that's what I am. I know

I'm attracted to women, but every time I imagine the two dudes in his books getting it on, my cock doesn't seem to give a shit. The gay porn thing didn't work out for me either. I'm not confused about my feelings for Julian, but I am confused about what's happening to me.

Waking up my computer, I decide to try to do a little research about myself. There's got to be people like me out there. Sure, I could just ask Julian what the hell is happening, but he doesn't seem to understand that the only man I'm attracted to is him. I don't even know what to search to make this make sense, so I try *being attracted to one person,* and hit *enter,* scouring the results.

I read into demisexuality, but it doesn't really fit for me. I do experience primary sexual attraction. I've hooked up with too many females without knowing them and enjoyed it. Sure, Julian and I bonded a bit, but I felt my attraction to him quickly.

I scroll down, clicking on an article about pansexuality, but that doesn't really apply either. I'm technically attracted to both sexes, I guess, but only Julian in the male category. Another nope there.

Then pops up an article that makes the most sense, heteroflexible. It says that it's a situational sexual behavior that's categorized by minimal homosexual activity, despite being straight. I read multiple stories about people that label themselves as heteroflexible, and yeah this might be the closest thing that's going on with me, but it still doesn't really click.

Frustrated, I slam my laptop shut. Why do I need a label? Sure, I get how it can make you understand yourself better, and I wish it was that easy for me, but it's not. It's just Julian. No one else. I don't need a label to know how I feel about him. We are what we are, and that's all that needs to matter. Fuck labels, I don't need one.

Looking at the clock, I realize it's already almost lunch time. Since I'll be with Julian after work, I'll just use my lunch hour to call my mom. It's been a while since I've last talked to her. Getting up from my desk, I close the door. She answers on the first ring, like she's been waiting for my call.

"Hey Mom, how are you doing?" I ask, sitting back in my desk chair.

"Oh, you know—same old, same old. It's been too long since you called me. I was starting to get worried," she says, sighing loudly into the phone, letting me know exactly how she feels about my lack of communication.

"Yeah, I've just been busy with work and stuff."

"Well, I was just thinking I'm due for a visit. What do you say? I don't have anything going on, and I would like to see you. It's been way too long."

"Yeah, whenever you want to come is fine. I can take off work."

"Let me pull up some flights right now while I have you since you *never call me,*" she says in a condescending voice.

"I know I've been slacking on the phone calls recently. I get it," I groan.

"Just because you're busy at work doesn't mean you can't call me after work, you know. Unless there's a lucky lady that's occupying all your time," she says with a chuckle.

"Actually, there's a lucky man," I say bluntly.

Holy shit. I didn't expect those words to fly out of my mouth, but they did. I can't take them back now.

"*Or man,*" she repeats, unphased. "How about this flight? It lands at 6:00 in the evening, you'll be off work by then, right?"

"Yeah, that's fine."

"Okay! Great! I'll book it right now!" she says excitedly.

"Um, Mom…you have nothing to say about me being with a man?"

"Nope. Whatever makes you happy, but I want to meet him when I come."

I can hear clanging in the background, like she's doing the dishes. The fact that I'm dating a man doesn't even stop her from *doing the dishes?*

"You really don't care, like at all?" I question.

"Why would I care? Use condoms."

"*Mom!* I'm not thirteen years old, I don't need to have *the talk.*"

"Well, you're sure acting like it. I figured you may have forgotten."

"Alright Mom, I'm on my lunch break. Text me the flight info when you book it," I say, trying to end this weird conversation.

"Sounds good! Love you! And can't wait to meet the lucky *mannn,*" she says, drawing out the word way too long before hanging up.

What. The. Fuck.

That was way too easy. Why was that so easy?

I've heard about horrible parents who shun their kids for being gay, and mine doesn't even bat a freaking eyelash? My mom is the most laid-back, accepting person in the world, so it shouldn't be surprising that she took the whole thing in stride. But damn, not even like, an awkward silence?

Popping my earbuds back in and hitting *play*, I get back to work. There are just a few hours until I meet Julian's Mom again. Hopefully, this time I can make a good impression. I'm going to delete that porn app, ASAP.

*****

"Whatever you're cooking smells delicious," I say while walking through Julian's door.

I could smell Italian food all the way down the stairs. My mouth is salivating at the smell.

I'm greeted with a big smile from Diana. "Pasta fagioli. One of my many specialties!" She beams.

"Where's Nora?" I ask, looking around the living room.

"She had some charity thing tonight," Julian replies. "That's what she does; she hosts large events for several charities. I think tonight is rescue animals," he says with a shrug. "But she should be back soon."

"You two go sit. Dinner will be ready soon!" Diana says, shooing us into the living room.

I sit next to Julian on the couch, placing my arm around the back of the seat. "I promise, no porn apps this time," I whisper into his ear with a chuckle.

He leans into my arm, burrowing himself into me with a sigh. It's been a few days since I've seen him and having him tuck into me like this instantly relieves all the stress that has accumulated. I'm left feeling light and free. I want him. I want him in every way. I want him to bury himself inside me and live there, but I also want his sadness, his hope, his fears. I want every part of him.

We stay like that, him burrowed into my side while I run my fingers through his hair. We don't talk, and we don't need to. Instead, we soak each other up until Diana announces that dinner is ready. I could sit on that couch all night, just me and him and the feeling of being perfectly complete.

Walking to the table to a spread of food we will never be able to finish, my mouth instantly waters. "Wow. This looks amazing Diana."

"You know, Julian loves my cooking. I'll teach you a thing or two to keep him happy," she says with a wink.

Sitting down, I begin placing heaping amounts of food on my plate. I didn't eat my lunch today, so my eyes are probably bigger than my stomach.

"Liam, we didn't have much time to get to know each other the last time we met. Julian hasn't told me, how did you two meet?" she asks, loading her plate with salad.

"I changed my number, and he accidentally texted it," I answer, looking over at Julian.

I'm not sure how much he wants to tell her. I'm not sure if he's still embarrassed about the way we met. It's a great story, in my opinion. It's the kind of epic story you tell your grandchildren one day.

"Yeah, I was texting James, and Liam got his old phone number," he says with a laugh.

Diana sits back in her chair, her hand flying to her chest. "So, wait. You were talking to James through text messages, and you were accidentally texting Liam? Right?" she asks, looking between us for confirmation.

"Yep," I answer, taking a bite of garlic bread.

"That's the best love story I've ever heard! How romantic!" she coos, her eyes watering like she might cry. "Julian, more salad," she scolds, picking up the tongs and adding more to his plate.

My eyes dart to Julian's when I hear the word *love* come out of his mother's mouth. *Love.* Is that what this is? Is this what love feels like? If this is what love is, I want it all the time. I want to roll around in it and soak up every single morsel of it.

"Oh God, that smells so freaking good," Nora says, walking through the door. "I hope there's some left. I haven't eaten all day."

"There's so much food here, we could feed an army. Sit down," Julian replies, kicking out a chair for her.

"Guess who I ran into?" Nora asks while piling her plate with pasta. "You'll never guess. Steven!"

"Oh, really? How is he doing?" Julian questions with his mouth full of food.

"He seemed alright," Nora answers with a shrug.

"Steven was James's best friend," Julian informs me with sadness in his eyes. "Anyway, let's not talk about James," he mutters, looking down at his plate.

"No, it's okay. I don't mind," I say while looking at Julian.

"Really?" he asks, the sadness in his voice changing to hope.

"Of course not. James is a part of you. He will always be a part of you," I explain.

I don't care if he talks about James. In fact, I want him to talk about James. I want to know everything about Julian, and James is a part of his story, and most importantly, a part of his heart.

"That's so sweet," Diana says, putting a comforting hand on my back. "Keep this one around Jules. He's a good one." She smirks, giving me a wink.

"I plan on it," he admits, looking up from his plate.

He plans on keeping me around? The thought of it makes my heart quicken its pace. I want so badly to be *kept around.*

We finish eating dinner, laughing and talking like a normal everyday family. I've never felt a sense of family like this, and I didn't realize how much I wanted it until now. The feeling of having people in your life who mean the world to you. The feeling of being comfortable in your own skin. The feeling of being loved. The feeling of home.

CHAPTER 33

"Movie Night!" Nora screams at the top of her lungs after my mom leaves. "But first, we clean up this mess," she says, getting up from her chair.

"I'll wash, you dry," Liam announces, pointing to Nora.

"I'll be in there in a minute," I groan, putting my hand on my stomach for dramatic effect. "I'm so full I can't move."

I watch from the couch as Nora and Liam get started, filling up the sink with water. Nora turns on the music app on her phone, blaring pop music while Liam laughs at her dancing next to him. I watch with fascination, remembering when James was still alive. All three of us, hanging out and laughing together. Just like this. I used to think that if I was with someone else, that person would take James' place. Liam isn't here to replace James, and he never will. My heart will always hold a piece of James, but my heart is big enough for both of them.

"This is my jam!" I hear Nora yell from the kitchen, the music suddenly getting louder, bringing me out of my thoughts.

Nora starts singing while shaking her ass in the air, using the countertop to keep from toppling over while Liam laughs at her. He starts singing along with her, using a spatula as a microphone. He's bumping his hip into her side and laughing, pure happiness on both of their faces.

Getting up to join them, I come up behind Liam, wrapping my arms around him as he laughs and sings with my best friend. Nora grabs a handful of soap from the sink, blowing it at me, making a big bubble of soap land on my face. Liam lets out a boisterous laugh that ripples through me, making my entire body buzz and surge with happiness.

In this moment, dancing with Nora and Liam, I realize my world is being spun off its axis, because I am falling in love. And not just a little bit. I'm falling in a *my life has officially changed forever kind of love.* I turn Liam around, pulling him into a searing kiss, one that I try to pour every single one of my emotions into.

Appreciation. Affection. Awe.

"Ugh! Get a room!" Nora interrupts, smacking us in the face with a dishtowel.

"Gladly," I reply, grabbing Liam's hand.

"No way! You are not getting out of these dishes," she snaps, holding onto my shirt sleeve.

"But you just said!" I whine.

"I take it back, now get to work," she says, handing me a dish.

After the dishes are all cleaned up, we settle onto the couch for a movie. I sit next to Liam, snuggling into his side. He puts his arm around my shoulder, letting me nestle into him even more. He lets out a sigh above me, like nothing else matters but this very moment.

Fishsticks wakes from his nap on the countertop, trotting his way toward us. He jumps up on Liam's lap, making biscuits and purring before settling in and making himself comfortable. Liam strokes his back gently. Fishsticks has clearly chosen Liam as his person, and I think I have too.

"Look at you, getting all those biscuits," I say, pointing to Fishsticks. "I get murder muffins."

"*Murder muffins?*" he asks, his head tilting to the side.

"Angry biscuits," I scoff, putting my hands out like claws.

"You leave Fishsticks alone. Do we have popcorn?" Liam asks, looking at Nora beside me. "Don't tell me I'm stuck watching *Pretty Woman,* and I don't even get popcorn."

"Get up and make it yourself. I'm not your maid," she sneers, glancing at my foot on her thigh. "And get your damn feet off me. No one likes feet, Jules."

"A lot of people love feet," I say, lifting my foot up. "In fact, there are people out there on the internet who make a damn good living off their feet."

"Gross," she mumbles, her face contorting into a grimace.

I lift myself out of Liam's embrace. "I'll get the damn popcorn."

"Extra butter! And don't burn it this time," Nora barks.

"*One time!* I burned it *one time* three years ago, and you'll never let me hear the end of it!"

"I would love to help you, but I have this affectionate cat in my lap," Liam says sarcastically, motioning to Fishsticks.

"It's *one* button. It even says *popcorn* on it. Don't fuck it up," Nora hisses.

"You're both insufferable," I huff out.

I make my way to the kitchen to make popcorn for the man I'm falling in love with and my asshole best friend. I'd say life is pretty damn good.

LIAM

CHAPTER 34

"Wakey, wakey. Hands off snakey," I say, whispering in Julian's ear, trying to wake him up. Giving him another nudge, I repeat a little louder this time, "Wakey, wakey. Hands off snakey," poking him with my finger.

He starts to stir, letting out a moan. Opening one eye, he glares at me. "I don't need my hands on my snakey when you're in my bed," he says with a chuckle, grabbing my ass and pulling me into his chest.

"Why do potatoes make good detectives?" I ask him, trying to keep him awake.

"It's too early for vegetable jokes," he murmurs.

"Because they keep their eyes peeled!" I whisper shout.

"You're insane."

"Insane about you," I respond, my face becoming serious. I lean up on one elbow, looking down at his sleepy face. "I've never been in love, Julian," I admit with honesty I've never set free. "I...I'm in awe of us, of the way we feel together. We fit, and I've never fit with anyone the way I fit with you."

He stares into my eyes, and by the look he's giving me, a verbal response isn't necessary. His eyes tell me everything I need to know. Cupping my chin, he rubs my cheek back and forth slowly, tears forming in his eyes.

"What? Did I say something wrong?" I ask hesitantly.

"No, no," he mutters, shaking his head back and forth. "I feel it too, Liam. I feel it too. Right here," he admits, putting my hand on his chest.

A single tear falls from his eye, slowly running down his cheek. I catch it with my thumb, "Then what's this?"

"Is this too good to be true? I don't deserve two happily ever afters," he confesses, his eyes darting away from me.

"Julian," I croak, pulling him closer to me. He buries his face in my chest, letting out a small soft sob.

"I'm here for you, and I promise I'll be here whenever you need me. I won't try to fix you, but I'll be here to help you make peace with your broken pieces," I vow, running my fingers through his hair.

He lets out a loud groan that vibrates in my chest. Words are no longer needed. We don't need anything but each other.

When I rub his back slowly and kiss the top of his head, he sits up and straddles me, taking in every part of my face. "Are you still not gay?" he asks with a cheeky grin.

"No, I'm not gay. I don't know what I am, and I honestly don't care. When I'm with you, and it feels like this, that's all that matters to me," I promise him, bringing his mouth in for a kiss.

I can taste the salt from his few tears on my lips, and I drink them in, trying to take away every ounce of pain. It hits me, this feeling in my chest. He doesn't just feel like home. He feels like everything.

"I believe you," he whispers against my mouth, making my heart soar in my chest.

Pulling him on top of me, I break off the kiss. "Is there room in there for me?" I ask, touching his heart with my palm. "Can you spare a sliver for me in this heart of yours? I'll never take James' spot, and I don't want to, but I need to know if you can carve out a piece for me, too."

"You're already in there, Liam. You've already got your own spot, right there. Only you," he reveals, rubbing my hand against his chest.

Bending down, he kisses me, nibbling on my jaw and my neck. He's making promises with his kisses, turning my whole world upside down.

"Fuck Julian, you're killing me," I whisper, running my hands up the back of his neck.

Seeking friction, I slowly roll up into him. Our cocks rubbing against each other just the right way, making me shudder with pleasure.

"God, you feel so good," I groan.

Pulling back, I look into his deep blue eyes. "I want all of you, Julian," I whisper softly "I want the things I read about in your books."

Butterflies flip flop in my stomach at my request, making my entire body buzz at the words.

"You want...you want to bottom? Or top?" he asks, raising his eyebrows.

"I don't know what any of that means," I say nervously. "I want you inside me. I want all of you. Every single bit of you. Everything you can give me," I say, my eyes flicking to his while my thumb moves across his cheek.

"Are you sure?" he asks.

"I'm not scared of this. I'm not scared of us," I mutter, taking his mouth in for another kiss.

I work my tongue into his mouth slowly, moaning into him when our tongues finally meet. My hands dust over his chest, making their way to his cock. I stroke him gently between us, making him grunt and moan into my mouth.

He reaches over to find the condoms and lube in the nightstand. When he does, he drops them onto the bed next to us.

"Like last time," he says, leaning back on his knees between my legs and lubing up his finger.

My back arches when his finger enters my hole, making him gasp at the sight of me. Fuck. I could get drunk off that sound.

"That's it, baby. You're doing so well for me," he says, encouraging me, praising me, making my eyes roll into the back of my head.

He works his way in and out slowly before adding more lube and another finger. He's going painfully slow. I need more.

"More. More please, more," I beg before he adds a third finger.

He scissors them back and forth. He hits my prostate and starts to open me up, making my balls draw up with need.

"Fuck, when I finally get inside of you, I'm not going to last a minute," he says, ripping the condom wrapper open with his teeth.

I watch him roll it on slowly. His eyes never waver from mine.

"You ready, baby? You ready to take my cock deep inside that pretty ass of yours?" he rasps.

"Yes." I nod.

I can't wait to give this to him. I want to give him all of me.

He gets on his knees and bends mine slightly, lining himself up to my entrance. Slowly, he eases just the tip inside of me, making me grunt at the sudden intrusion.

"Breathe, baby. Breathe," he encourages. My pulse racing, he moves forward just another inch. "Tell me if it's too much. Tell me if I need to stop."

"Keep going," I let out on a sigh, trying to relax myself.

My hands move to his hips possessively, pushing him deeper inside. It's uncomfortable as hell right now, but my experience doing this with females tells me it won't be soon. I know Julian will make it perfect.

He looks down and at our cocks. Mine is hard and ready against my abs, and his is inside of me. "Fuck. Look at you taking me so well," he grits out through his teeth. "Look at you. You're doing so fucking good for me."

He pumps his hips forward until he's buried deep inside of me. I let out a loud yelp, yanking him by the back of his neck so we're chest to chest. Leaning forward on his elbows, he slowly thrusts into me.

"Nothing has ever felt as good as you do right now," he whispers while he moves his lips over my neck, barely dusting my pounding pulse point. "God, you're so perfect, so perfect for me."

He runs his hands down my sides, making goosebumps erupt all over my arms. "Look how well you take my cock. Like you were fucking made for it," he says while he sits up, putting my knees on top of his thighs while he ruts up into me. Leaning his head back, he moans with pleasure. Taking ahold of my hard cock, he strokes me, faster and faster until I'm withering and sputtering.

"Fuck. It's yours. So full. So full of you," I mumble incoherently.

"Damn right it's mine," he responds possessively.

My cock twitches and my balls draw up at his words. Just the word *mine* almost sends me over the edge.

"Julian, God," I breathe as he hits my prostate, feeling my climax getting closer.

"That's it. I need you to come for me, baby," he says urgently. "Your ass is squeezing me so tight, I'm about to lose control."

Everything is amplified in this very moment. The sounds of his moans. The feel of his hands. My senses are heightened one thousand percent, making my world turn upside down. Stars dance beneath my eyelids, my rhythm becoming erratic.

"Yesss," I rasp out before I come all over our chests and his hand.

He pauses when I come, watching me and letting me come down from my climax before thrusting into me two more times. He comes, whimpering and panting while I watch. There is nothing I love more than watching him be pleasured by me. It's intoxicating that I'm able to do this to him.

He removes himself from me slowly, making me groan at the feeling of emptiness. Tying off the condom and throwing it in the trash, he starts putting his jeans back on. "Stay right there," he tells me with a stern tone.

He comes back with a warm rag, slowly cleaning up my chest. "Are you okay?" he asks, raking his eyes all over my body. "Did I hurt you? Does anything hurt?"

"No. It was perfect," I answer, dragging him into another kiss.

I swear I'm drowning. I'm fucking drowning in him.

"On all fours. I'm going to make you feel better," he says, grabbing my shoulder and pushing me over.

I do as he asks, getting up on my knees and putting my ass up in the air.

Situating himself behind me, he kisses both of my cheeks. "You were so good, baby," he says before swiping his tongue up my crack slowly. "And now I'm going to show you just how much I loved it. Come over here, and sit that ass on my face," he orders, putting his legs between mine and laying down. I sit up, putting my ankles under his arms and putting my arms on his legs to hold myself up.

His tongue darts straight into my hole, soothing the sting there. I shift myself to where I want him to be.

"Juliannnn, oh fuck," I gasp while he licks my tender hole.

"This ass is mine," he murmurs, pulling his hand back and smacking it.

"Fuck," I groan, my ass stinging.

He whips his hand back, smacking it again while his tongue works its magic. Who knew I got off by being spanked?

"Again," I mewl.

I had no idea how much I'd enjoy being spanked. My is cock is rock hard again. I give it a single stroke, trying to get some relief.

"Julian, I need to come again," I growl.

"Yeah, baby. Fucking cover me with it," he demands, licking me faster.

Looking down, I notice Julian's cock is hard and ready again, bouncing against his abs as he devours me. Leaning down, I take him in my hand and take the tip of him into my mouth, whirling my tongue around him and tasting him. He bucks up into my mouth, demanding more.

"Fuck yeah. You're so good at that. Such a quick learner," he rasps out.

I take him down to the base of his shaft, moaning around his cock and cupping his balls gently. I bob my head up and down to keep pace with him while his tongue darts in and out of my hole. He's shuddering below me, moaning so loud against me that it vibrates through my entire body.

"I'm gonna..." he yells.

Sitting up, I jack him furiously until he comes again. My hand is covered with him. I swipe his release off his stomach and grab my own cock, not able to hold it back any longer.

Stroking myself above him, he sticks a finger in my hole, hitting my prostate and sending me reeling. I come so hard I lose my balance, my head tilted back in a silent scream. He moans into me when my hot come hits his stomach, mixing with his.

"Yeah, baby. Yeah. That's it," he hums with encouragement.

My chest heaving, my body totally spent, I fall on top of him while he moves out from underneath me. I stare in awe as he cleans himself up and then flops down next to me on the bed.

"No sex has ever been like this. Nothing has ever been like this," I whisper.

"I know," he says, looking into my eyes.

He lies behind me, pulling my back into his chest and wrapping his arm around me. He tucks his face into the back of my neck and sighs.

"Thank you, Julian," I whisper, so softly I can barely hear my own words.

"For what?"

"For letting me in," I mumble just before I fall back asleep.

CHAPTER 35

After Liam leaves, I head straight to my computer. I have an idea in my head, and I need to get it down. I think I can officially say I've got my groove back. I spend hours in front of my laptop, almost halfway through a rough draft of a story about two guys who find each other after the death of a husband, just like Liam and I. Turns out my mom was right. Falling in love can really inspire a person.

When my eyes are so heavy that I can't keep them open, I make my way to the kitchen for a snack and find Nora working at the kitchen table.

"Well, good to see you, too. You've been in that hole of yours for hours," she states.

"Writing," I blurt out.

Looking up from her laptop, she smiles. "Hope it doesn't suck."

"Thanks for all the support," I respond sarcastically, opening the fridge.

A new *Post-It Note* is attached to the handle:

NEVER BUY WHEATGRASS AGAIN. IT'S DISGUSTING.

"You try wheatgrass in your smoothies?" I ask, pointing to the note.

"I don't want to talk about it. It was a catastrophe, and I gagged a lot."

Fishsticks opens his eyes and stares at me from the countertop. Standing up and stretching, he lets out a hiss in my direction. I must have pissed him off at some point in the last five business days.

"How is he doing?" I ask, pointing to Fishsticks.

"He's still an asshole."

"No shit," I say, shaking my head.

"Except for when Liam is here," she adds with a smile.

"Speaking of Liam...." I sigh, sitting down across from her at the kitchen table.

"Don't tell me you've fucked this up already," she scoffs while rolling her eyes.

"He says he's not gay," I admit.

"Well, I heard you two this morning, and I'd definitely say he's in denial about that," she says with a laugh.

"No, that's not what I meant," I say, trying to explain the situation the best I can. "I mean, he says he's only attracted to me."

"You mean, like, that he's not attracted to other males?" she asks, putting her chin in her hand.

"Yeah. Is that weird?"

"No," she shrugs, looking back down at her computer screen.

"Really? You don't think that's strange?"

"He's attracted to what's inside of you, not what's outside of you," she assures me.

"I'd definitely say he's attracted to what's outside of me," I say with a laugh.

"Ugh. That's not what I meant, perv," she says, shaking her head. "I think it's special. The romantic in me is swooning right now," she says, putting her hand over her heart.

If we were in a cartoon, she'd have literal hearts in her eyes. Those rom-coms have made her so sappy.

"What do you think about...James? Have you thought about him at all lately?" I ask hesitantly.

"Of course, I have. Just because Liam's here doesn't mean I don't miss him," she says with a scowl on her face. "You have got to give up the idea that being with someone else replaces him. He's a part of you, and he will always be loved by you."

"And what do you think he would think of all this?" I ask, waving my hand around the room.

She looks up from her laptop, giving me a pointed stare. "I want you to be surrounded by love. I think that's what James would want too."

"Yeah? You think he would like Liam?" I ask hopefully.

"Yeah, I do. Liam is good, even I can see that. Have you talked to James lately? And *not* over text message?" she chuffs.

"Yeah. Kinda. A little bit. No," I answer truthfully.

"Don't be a creeper this time. Just go to his grave," she snaps.

"Yeah, I'll go. I know I don't go enough," I say, standing up.

"Hey, let's have a game night like we used to. Invite Liam?"

"Yeah, fine, but not *Monopoly*. You're a sadist. We don't need Liam to see you in that state. Not yet, you'll scare him off."

"Hey! I take *Monopoly* very seriously!"

"Trust me, I'm well aware! You almost broke the coffee table last time!" I yell, walking back into my dungeon.

Sitting at my desk, I think back to when I came out. How hard it was for me. Even though I have great people in my life, I repressed it and denied it, even to myself. And here's Liam, going all in without a care in the world, not antagonizing over it in the slightest. He says he's not gay, and I believe that. It's just me, and that makes me fly head over heels for him even more. It's *just me* and my heart soars in my chest at the thought. It's like fate swooped into our lives, completely blindsiding us both. All this time I thought fate dealt me a bad hand of cards, but the tables have turned, and I now hold a royal flush.

*****

"I don't come here often enough," I say, looking at James' headstone.

It's nothing fancy, just his name and the dates that always accompany headstones. Looking down I notice flowers have been planted next to it. They're still in bloom, and the dirt around them is freshly dug, meaning Nora has been here recently.

"Nora is better at this stuff than I am," I mutter under my breath, crunching the leaves under my feet. "I'm sorry, I know I don't come here very much."

I feel like an idiot talking to a headstone. I know it's a perfectly normal thing to do, but this isn't James. This is just a marker telling me where he's buried. Glancing around the graveyard, I make sure no one's around to hear me. The only person here is an old man raking leaves. I'm sure he sees people talking to graves all the time.

"So...." I say, looking up to the sky. "Sorry I didn't bring flowers," I add, laughing out loud.

James didn't even like flowers. He wouldn't care about flowers by his grave. The only reason he even has a grave is because his mother insisted. I would have been fine with cremation and spreading him somewhere like the beach or the top of a mountain. Anywhere besides this place full of loss and sorrow. This place is just depressing.

"I don't know if you're up there watching or not...but, I'm seeing someone," I say, sitting down on my knees.

I start plucking out the few sprigs of grass that are protruding on the sides of his headstone making it look nicer. I know Nora comes out here and keeps it nice and tidy.

"I think you would like him," I admit with a small smile.

"It's been so hard without you, James. So hard," I gasp.

I feel my eyes starting to well up with tears. Taking a breath, I try to hold them back. I'm so tired of crying. You'd think as much as I've cried, there wouldn't be any tears left in me. I should be all dried up by now.

"I thought... well, I thought that I couldn't be with someone else after I lost you, but I think I can," I whisper. "I've realized that life ends, but love doesn't. I'll never stop loving you," I stammer, my voice trembling. "You were the man I loved when I had you. Liam can be the man I love in a world without you," I confess grabbing my chest, a small sob escaping my throat. I swallow over the tears, trying to keep them in.

Standing up and dusting off my knees, I look up at the sky, tears slowly falling down my cheeks. "My heart was half-empty without you here. I'm going to let Liam fill it up again."

I make my way slowly out of the bleak graveyard, looking at all the lonely gravestones. There are people out there just like me. People who have learned to live without the people they love. People who felt like the world was swallowing them up. I hope that those people who have loved and lost have learned to find love again.

CHAPTER 36

JULES: Nora wants to have game night tonight. Do you wanna join?

ME: I can't. I promised a work friend I'd go out with him tonight.

JULES: It's for the best. Nora is ruthless.

ME: I'm down for next week. Me and you against Nora. We'll kick her ass.

JULES: So down.

I promised Oscar I'd be his wingman tonight. If I cancel, he will lose his shit. I just have to get through tonight, and he'll be off my back for at least a week. I'm going to have to do something about this whole Oscar situation, and soon.

Swinging open the door to *Mixers*, I make my way up to an empty table, finding Oscar already swaying side to side up at the bar. Fuck. This is going to be a fun night. Oscar sober is one thing. Oscar drunk is a whole different level of intolerable.

Walking up to the bar, I shove his shoulder to get his attention. "Dude, I got us a table," I yell over the blaring music, pointing to the empty table I've claimed with my coat.

"I'll be over in a minute," he says, raising his eyebrows and cutting his eyes in the direction of the woman next to him.

Shaking my head, I order myself a beer and make my way across the bar when a woman intercepts me. I nod my head a few times to act like I'm listening before making an excuse to leave. I have no interest in anyone here. I'm taken, and damn it's never felt so good.

"Did you just turn her down? Did you *see* her?" Oscar yells, his hands flailing in the air.

"Yeah. I'm not interested," I say, shaking my head.

"Damn. This thing with Jules is really serious. Huh?"

"Yeah, man. I told you. I'm here to be your wingman, nothing more."

"More for me then," he preens with a smirk.

Sitting at the table while Oscar ogles women is about as exciting as watching paint dry. I tune him out as he drones on and on about whatever woman he took home last night and how hot she was, as if I want to hear all the sordid details. How can I get through to him that I just *don't care*?

"Look at that girl by the bar with the curly hair. She keeps looking our way. Do you know her?" he asks, ducking his head and pointing across the bar.

I look to my left to seem interested when I notice the woman that he's pointing at is none other than Nora. The man standing next to her is Julian.

No, no, no, no.

This is bad. *This is so bad.*

"Hey, man, I gotta go," I stutter.

I need to get out of here before Julian spots me. I don't need him and Oscar to be on the same planet, much less in the same room. Oscar is drunk which means he's going to make a scene. A scene I'm not ready for. The way he acted when that Brandon guy hit on me, I don't even want to speculate how *Drunk Oscar* would react to finding out I'm seeing Julian.

"She noticed me checking her out. She's on her way," he enthuses with a smile, leaning back in his chair.

Ducking my head, I look down at the table and pretend to scratch a nonexistent itch on my forehead to hide my face. How did I think I could ever avoid this situation to begin with? I'm an idiot.

"*Liam!*" Nora yells, waving her hand while walking toward me.

"You know her? Dude, hook me up! She's a hottie!" he whispers to me just before Julian and Nora get to our table.

"Liam, I didn't know you were coming here," Julian says, shoving his hands in his pocket. "Nora and her *friend* had a tiff. She wanted to get some drinks," he says, putting air quotes around the word *friend*.

"You going to introduce us or what?" Oscar says, gesturing to Nora.

"Nora, this is Oscar," I mutter under my breath.

"And I'm Jules," Julian says, sticking his hand out for Oscar to shake.

Oscar gapes at his hand suspended in midair. His mind works quickly for a drunk person.

"*Jules?*" he says, his expression wrinkled in confusion. "*Jules* as in *the Jules you're dating*?" he squawks, looking over at me as his face contorts in a way I've never seen before. It's part disgust, part confusion, part rage.

"Um...." Julian stammers quietly as Nora starts backing away.

"You're dating *a fucking man?*" Oscar yells, standing up from his stool so fast the legs skid against the floor. "You told me Jules was a *woman!*" he fumes, pointing at me.

Julian looks my direction, his face beat red. If you look up the definition of the word "shame" in the dictionary, it would be the description of Julian's eyes at this moment. The agony of his hurt courses through my own veins. I've fucked up...again. I've got to find a way to fix this before it gets out of control.

"You told...you said..." Julian stutters, tilting his head.

He can barely get his words out. He's just as speechless as I am. I can't figure out a way to fix this fast enough.

"What the fuck is wrong with you?" Oscar fumes, inching closer to me.

My eyes dart between Julian and Oscar. I can't decide which detrimental event to diffuse first. I glance at Nora, hoping she can give me some type of direction.

Fuck.

Why did I think she could throw me a lifeline? She's his best friend for a reason. Of course his pain is her pain, judging by the way her hand is clasped over her mouth, her eyes wide taking me in like I've grown three heads. She grabs the back of Julian's shirt, attempting to rip him away from the scene of the crime I've created. She's taking him away from me. The world I want is leaving, and I'm getting banished to one I want no part of anymore.

"No," I whisper, reaching my hand out for Julian.

He jerks his entire body away from me, spins around and books it toward the door. He doesn't even look back. He doesn't look back *once*.

I explode so fast that I can't stop myself. Grabbing Oscar by the front of his shirt, I plow him into the nearest wall.

"*You!* You *motherfucker!*" I roar, my face inches from his.

Bartenders and other patrons run in our direction. They're yelling at me to stop, attempting to split us apart. I don't hear their words. My focus is on Oscar and how he just royally fucked up my life.

"You're a fucking asshole," I yell into his face "And you aren't worth it," I growl with one final shove before letting him go.

"Are you for fucking real right now? Fucking shoving me?" he retorts, trying to shove me back. "What's so special about him that you're willing to throw your best friend to the side like a piece of garbage?"

"Everything! *Everything* about him is special. He's everything you're not, and everything you'll never be," I shout, pushing my finger into his chest before turning around to leave.

Yanking my coat off the back of the chair, I storm out of the bar that I was going to get kicked out of anyway. I don't know how I'm going to fix this mess, but the thought of not having Julian in my life feels like the way I imagine my mother felt when she lost my father.

CHAPTER 37

It's been a week since I saw Liam at the bar. It's been a week since I've left this bed. I'm back to the old habit of reminding myself to breathe.

Breathe in. Breathe out.

I gave Liam all the empty spaces of my heart, and now it's shattered into so many pieces that I'm surprised it's still beating. I'm surprised I don't need a pacemaker with all it's been through.

As if on a perfect schedule, the atrocious whirling and grinding begins. That fucking blender. "Damn it, Nora!" I bellow before stuffing my head under the pillow.

The pillow that no longer smells like Liam.

The pillow that no longer smells like James.

Here she comes, Nora and her dramatic stomps in 3....2....1...

She swings the door open so hard it slams into the wall behind it. "Hey, you! With the face!" she yells, wrenching the blankets off my body.

"Liam has been here three times, and you make me make him leave every single time. Next time, you're dealing with it," she roars, her finger jabbing into my chest.

Groaning, I roll over so my back is facing her. I don't even want to look at her right now. If I do, it means I have to face this disaster called *my life*.

"You're a hot ass mess. Look at you!"

"I'm not a hot mess! I'm a *spicy disaster!*" I bark, sitting up.

When I sit up, my hair doesn't move. It's so greasy that it's mashed to the side of my face. Yeah. I'm more than a spicy disaster.

Sitting down on the edge of the bed with a sigh, she breathes in and out, trying to calm herself down before continuing her tirade. She's really freaking mad this time.

"Okay, Jules, I get it. You're heartbroken, but I'm going to be honest with you because that's what I do best. I think you're overreacting."

"I'm *overreacting?*" I bellow. "Did you *see* his face? Did you see how ashamed he was of me? He was ashamed of *me*, Nora. Ashamed of *us!*" I shriek.

"I want you to think about when you came out. I want you to think about that right now. Picture it—*Sicily 2001*," she says, waving her hand in the air.

"Oh, don't you dare try to give me *Golden Girl* advice," I scoff, crossing my arms over my chest.

"Okay, then I'll speak for myself, you stubborn mule. There was always one person you didn't want to tell that you were gay, right? One person who you knew wouldn't take you coming out well, and you avoided telling them for as long as possible, right?" she says, nodding her head, trying to get me to agree with her.

"Yeah. I guess, but I was right. When my grandma finally found out, she banned me from Christmas." I sigh at the unpleasant memory.

"Well, that person for Liam was that Oscar guy at the bar, apparently. You need to get over it, or *I'm* going to ban *you* from Christmas."

"I can't Nora. I can't," I sputter. "I just can't get the picture of him out of my head. That look of shame on his face." I rub my eyes, trying to get the image out of it.

She raises her hand and smacks me across the side of the head. "There! Now it's out!"

"Hey, damn it! My heart was ripped out of my body at that moment. It's not that easy!" I defend, rubbing the side of my head.

"Jules—*ever the dramatic*." She chuckles.

"I was so heartbroken when James died, now I'm mourning someone who is alive."

"You don't have to. He's here trying to make this right if you'd just hear him out."

"Ugh! I can't!" I grunt, laying back down in bed.

"Oh, no you don't! Get out of this bed and wash your ass. You fuck-ing stink!" she screeches, tugging on my arm.

"Fine! But I'm only washing half of my ass!" I groan, hauling myself up.

"After your shower we can go get some greasy waffles. Comfort food. The food you eat when you're in mourning," she snarks with a laugh. "Oh, and Fishsticks needs his insulin. I'm tired of tackling that demon all by myself, so get the fuck up and help me," she demands before walking out.

Here I am. I'm back in the same situation I was two months ago. I'm heartbroken once again. Who knew you could mourn the living? I shouldn't have gone out in public and *people-d*. I should have never let Liam in. I did this to myself.

LIAM

CHAPTER 38

I have to pick up my mother from the airport, who has decided to come at the most inopportune time. I feel like a piece of shit and I can't even stand myself.

Julian refuses to let me fix my fuck-up. I've tried everything. I've tried to call him. I've sent so many messages I feel like a stalker in one of his true crime shows. I've even gone over to his apartment, only to have Nora boot me out. There's nothing left to do but drown myself in my sorrow. I've never experienced heartbreak before, and it's as bad as the love songs at *Mixers* say it is. It really fucking sucks.

Getting out of the car at the *arrivals* terminal, I find my mother standing with a large pink suitcase and three extra bags on top of it. Her sunglasses are way too big for her face, and her blonde hair is the size of Guam. It looks like she's going on a mid-life crisis cruise and plans on staying here for two months with all that crap.

Grabbing her rollaway, I bring her in for a tight hug. "Hey, Mom," I murmur into her hair.

"Why are you scowling like that? You'd think you'd be happier to see me. You look miserable," she says, pushing me away from her to take me in.

"We can talk about it later. C'mon." I grimace and start rolling her suitcase toward the car.

"We have about thirty minutes until we get to your apartment. That's all the time you get, then you better be happy again. I'm only here for a few days and don't want to see you looking like this the entire time," she says, glancing at the watch on her wrist.

I shove her suitcase into the trunk and stow the rest of her baggage in the back seat. "Why do you need all this stuff, Mom? Jesus," I mutter under my breath.

"You don't know my life!" she says, settling into the passenger seat.

As soon as I get behind the wheel, she wastes no time. "Now, what the hell is wrong with you? You look like bloody hell," she snaps, pulling the visor down and inspecting herself in the mirror.

"Me and my....well, boyfriend…broke up. I screwed up, Mom," I admit.

"Typical," she says, slamming the visor closed.

"Gee. Thanks," I sneer.

"You've never been good at that lovey dovey stuff. I blame your father. It took me years to get him to show his emotions. When I met him, he was like a statue. All stone. Could never get through to him," she chuckles.

"But you loved him anyway."

"Yep, and I'll never stop loving him," she says, her eyes boring into the side of my head as I make my way down the highway. "That doesn't mean you didn't inherit his gene of dispassion," she laments with a sigh, looking out her window.

"That's not a gene, Mom."

"Whatever helps you sleep at night," she says, waving her hand at me.

"Good talk," I say, glancing in her direction.

"So, what are our plans? You better get your shit together. I can't be around a Debbie Downer the entire week."

"I'll do my best," I huff.

"Well, as they say, *losers do their best, winners go home and fuck the prom queen*, or in your case....*king*," she adds with a laugh.

THE RIGHT WRONG NUMBER

"*No one* says that, Mom."

"Well, you're not a teenager anymore, Liam. You're a grown adult and a good man. I have faith that you'll figure it all out," she assures, resting her hand over top of mine, ultimately ending the conversation.

"I have to work tomorrow. I also have a charity event on Friday, so I hope you packed a nice dress in all those suitcases." I say, hitching my thumb toward the trunk.

"I didn't, but I can go shopping. You want to come with me?" she asks excitedly.

"No. Absolutely not," I say firmly.

"Oh, come on! Don't be a killjoy!"

"I'll leave you the car tomorrow. I am not going shopping with you," I say, shaking my head.

"You're just like your father," she says, letting out a heavy sigh. "If you didn't come out of my vagina, I would be concerned that you weren't mine."

"Again. Good talk."

Shit. I'm heartbroken, and I'm going to have to deal with this all week? I don't know if I'll make it out alive.

*****

I've been avoiding Oscar. I haven't spoken to him since I slammed him up against the wall at the bar. I didn't think I would lose my shit like that. Even though I shouldn't have, I'm not apologizing for it. His homophobic ass can go to hell.

"Hello," I answer, picking up my office phone.

"Come to my office," my boss barks on the other end.

"Be right there," I say, hanging up.

I don't know what I did, but Oscar better not have narc-ed me out for our little mishap. That happened off the clock, and it's none of my boss' business. He can't discipline me for that.

I make my way to his office, having to pass Oscar's on the way. I glance in and see him pounding away at his keyboard. He may have driven me crazy, but he's been my friend for years. I still feel a tinge of sadness at the loss of our friendship. Just a tinge. The rest is hate.

Walking into my boss' office, I sit down in the chair across from his desk. "What's up?" I ask nonchalantly.

"Charity event tonight. You know the deal," he informs me, handing me the formal invitation.

"My mom is in town," I say, wondering if there's any possibility of getting out of this.

I'm pissed off at the world. I'm not in the mood to bid on a date that I won't go on. I'm going to have to mingle...with people. I don't know if I'm up for it.

"She can be your plus-one," he says, tapping his desk. "No more than one thousand dollars on the date. You don't have to go on it, just do the bidding. If she's hot, maybe I'll take her on the date," he adds with a laugh.

"Got it. I'll handle it." I sigh, getting up to leave.

I make my way back to my office and find Oscar sitting in the seat across from my desk. I shut the door behind me, giving him a look of distrust. "What do you want?"

"I've come to apologize," he says on a defeated breath. "I was an asshole."

As much as I want to believe it, I find it hard to buy. A person as crass as Oscar doesn't just change their belief system overnight.

"Oh, yeah? You're really sorry, huh?" I ask sarcastically.

"Yeah, I am. I don't care if you're dating a man. It just caught me by surprise. We've been friends for years. You've never thought to tell me you were attracted to dudes?"

"It was a new development," I say, shrugging stiffly, feeling the sting that new is no longer shiny and new, but rather old and tarnished. Sighing, I scrub my face with my hands. "And it's over," I mutter as bitterly as I feel. "We aren't dating anymore."

"Because of me?" he asks, pointing to his chest.

"No. Because of me. I didn't tell you Jules was a man. I fucked up by letting you go on thinking he was a woman, so when he found that out…" I trail off, too ashamed to revisit the anguish in front of Oscar. "I'm sure your reaction didn't help my case though," I inform him, stacking up the papers beside me.

"Fuck man. I'm sorry," he huffs, shifting in the chair. "This was *new*? Like…you've *never* been with a man before?"

"Right. Just Julian." I sigh.

Just Julian. It will always be *just Julian*.

"Okay. Yeah. Okay. I was upset. I thought we were friends. I thought you could tell me stuff," he admits.

"It was just...complicated," I confess, finally looking up at him.

"I get it," he says, putting up his hands. "Totally. I do, s-so...are we cool?" he asks.

"Yeah, sure Oscar."

"You're still going to the charity thing tonight, right?"

"Yeah. My mom's in town, so I'm taking her."

"Cool. Are you sure we're okay? I promise I didn't mean to come off like that. I was just *surprised*. You know?"

"Yeah, we're good," I mutter.

He nods sheepishly and then makes his way out the door. I'm still mad at him. He acted like a complete asshole, but I have to work with him. I'll deal with him at work, and that's it. No more bar nights. No more playing wingman. I'm done.

I know the whole situation was my fault. I fucked up, and I should have told him Jules was a man. I didn't because I wanted to avoid the blow up I suspected would occur. I should have just told him.

I miss Julian so much, it's like the air has been sucked out of me. My bones will never let me forget him. They won't forget the way they felt when our hands were intertwined. They won't forget what they felt like when he was snuggled up next to me. They won't forget the way they felt when he was on top of me, around me, inside me.

The image of Julian with someone else floods my mind. Him on top of another man. Him sliding into someone else and whispering, *"Look at you."* Him with his praising voice, telling someone else how good they're doing for him. Him with his tongue whirling around someone else's cock.

I need a fucking lobotomy after those images flash though my brain, because thinking of Julian with someone sends a shard of pain through my chest that almost brings me to my knees.

JULES

CHAPTER 39

Running down the hallway and into the living room, I find Nora scribbling something on a bright pink *Post-It Note*. It's probably about hummus this time. There is every type of hummus stacked in our refrigerator right now. You'd think she'd learn that this healthy shit tastes terrible.

"I finished the book!" I shout, beaming from ear to ear.

I'm sporting the first smile I've had in over a week. I have to massage my facial muscles. I swear they haven't been in the upright position since I saw Liam at the bar.

"You finished it? Already?" she asks, her brows hitching up.

"Turns out heartbreak is a great form of inspiration. Who knew?" I say, reaching into the cupboard for a cup.

"Wow. Let me call Liam and have him break your heart again then. Imagine how many books you could write?" She laughs.

"Shut up, you heathen," I huff, pouring myself a shot of tequila.

I always drink a shot of tequila after I finish writing a book. That's the rule. Can't break traditions, ya know?

"Listen, I need a favor," Nora says, sitting down at the table.

"No. No favors! This has been the best day I've had in over a week, please don't ruin it," I whine, pinching my eyes closed.

"Pretty please, with chocolate on top, and ice cream in the middle?" she begs, putting her hands together and sticking her lower lip out.

"That's not how that goes," I grunt in annoyance, begrudgingly taking the seat across from her.

"You owe me, Jules!" she exclaims.

"I do not owe you," I argue, crossing my arms over my chest.

"But...but...I've been giving Fishsticks his insulin *all by myself*," she pouts.

True. She has, and I certainly don't feel like dealing with that task again until I absolutely have to.

"Fine. What?" I ask with a huff.

"I have this work event tonight, and well, someone canceled..." she says, clicking away at her laptop.

"And why is that my problem?"

"You don't want your very best friend to suffer, do you?"

"Wrong question to ask me," I sneer. "Fine. What do I have to do? Fold napkins and shit?"

"Well, not exactly. You see, I'm down a man for the auction."

"Auction..." I say warily.

"A date auction," she says softly, her bottom lip sticking out.

"No. No. No. No. Absolutely not. *Hell no*. Nope," I rant, getting up from my chair.

"Okay. Pretty please with a cherry on top?" she begs again, this time making tears well up in her eyes.

"Quit making yourself cry! I know your dirty tricks, woman! I know you can do that on command!"

"Come on, Jules! I'm begging you! I have no one else to fill the spot last minute like this."

"Fine. Fucking fine, but then you owe me after this!" I yell. "You're doing all the chores for a week!" If there's anything Nora hates more than I hate green smoothies, it's cleaning. The minute I say the word *chores,* she'll start backpedaling.

"A week? Oh, come on, Jules!"

"A week, or no deal."

"Ugh, fine!" she grouses, slamming her hand on the table. "Now, go wash your ass, no one likes a stinky date."

"More of a reason *not* to shower," I deadpan. "Fuck, Nora. I *really* don't want to do this."

"I'll be there the whole time. I promise. There are free drinks!" she exclaims.

"Good because I'm going to have to get a serious buzz before getting on that stage to be bid on. It just feels sleezy," I say, shaking my head.

"People love it. We make tons of money for great causes. All those old ladies in the audience eat it up." She laughs.

"Old ladies? You're just making this sound better and better," I say sarcastically.

I make my way back to my room to dig out my tuxedo to wear for this freakshow. I am being forced to go out on a date with an old lady who will probably paw me to death while smelling like mothballs and *Polygrip*. I could find so many things I'd rather do with my time. Like trying to pet Fishsticks. Or falling into a pit of ravenous turtles. Or getting a root canal...without *Novocain*.

Yeah. Any of those things would be better than this.

LIAM

CHAPTER 40

I walk into the charity event with my mother on my arm. It took her four hours to pick the red dress she has on. It also took her four hours to get ready, hence why I'm walking in the door almost an hour late. Finding my boss in the corner with a glass of scotch in his hand, I hustle over to him to let him know I'm here. I need credit when it's due.

"I've made it," I huff.

"Better late than never," he says, glancing at his watch. "And who is this lovely lady?" he asks, his smile ten times larger than it was a minute ago.

"This is Mary, my mother," I say sternly.

He is not going to hit on my mother like a sleaze ball. There are plenty of other women in his age group at this function. In fact, that's all there is. Glancing around the room, I notice ninety percent of tonight's guests would qualify for a senior citizen discount.

Mom extends her hand extra gracefully. Why the fuck is she acting all fancy? Nope. This isn't happening.

"Lovely to meet you too," she coos with a charming smile.

And that's enough of that. I tug on her arm. "Let's go get a drink," I whisper. For good measure I add, "Open bar."

I want her to be as far away from my boss as possible. There is no way I'm going to sit here and watch this.

"Free drinks?" she exclaims, letting go of my boss' hand.

We make our way to the bar, finding Oscar already half-drunk and hanging on a bleach blonde dressed in a midnight blue dress. He's drunk, again. *Great.*

"Hey, man," I say, pushing his shoulder to get his attention.

I may still be kind of mad at him, but I'll stay cordial for the sake of my job. As my mother would say, I am great at keeping my feelings buried.

"Thought you weren't going to show!" he yells, turning in my direction.

Holding onto my mother's arm, I cock my head to the side. "This is my mom. Mom, this is Oscar."

"I've heard so much about you!" she says with a cheeky grin.

She sure has, and not all good like he believes.

Grabbing two champagne flutes off the bar, I ask, "Alright, when does this thing start?"

Looking around the room, I notice the podium is all set up and the auctioneer is shuffling through some papers. Once we get this show on the road, I can get out of here. This event can't end soon enough.

"Anytime. It was supposed to start about ten minutes ago," Oscar informs me.

"Let's go find our table," I mutter, tapping my mother's shoulder.

Walking around, we finally find our place cards and sit in our assigned seats just as the auctioneer starts her speech. Oscar is to my right, and my mother on my left as my plus-one.

"Can I have everyone's attention!" the auctioneer says, tapping on the microphone. "It's time to start the auction!" she adds while everyone settles in their seats around us.

"The rules are simple! The highest bidder gets a date with one of our lucky ladies or our handsome gentleman!" she yells, clapping her hands. "We will start with the gentlemen!" she adds, winking at the old ladies in the front row.

Out comes a line of gentlemen, strutting their way across the stage, all up for bids. "Want any of those hunks?" I mutter to my mother, taking a drink of my champagne.

"Hmmmm...." she hums, tapping her chin. "They're all too old for me, except that one right there," she adds, pointing to the left end of the stage.

I look up to locate the man she's pointing at. When I see who she's singled out, my face slackens.

It's *Julian.*

My Julian is up on that stage and up for bids. I find Nora at the end, directing the contestants into a straight line.

"Here is gentleman number-one!" she shouts into the microphone. "Bill here is a thrill-seeker," she reads off the card in front of her, "but loves to cozy up next to a fire with a good movie! Which one of you lovely ladies would like to cozy up next to Bill?" she asks. "The bidding starts at one hundred dollars!"

Looking around the room, I see five hands shoot up for a cozy-up with Bill. My gaze moves to Julian. He's completely unaware that I'm in the audience. He fiddles with the hem of his suit jacket nervously, eyes constantly darting toward Nora. I'm happy to see that he doesn't look like he wants to be here.

The next two gentlemen get bid, but my only focus on that stage is Julian. Watching his fingers fidget back and forth, my eyes can't stray far from his anxious face.

"He's mine," I finally whisper to my mother next to me.

She flashes me a confused look, so I clear my throat and clarify, "That's the man I was seeing."

Her hand darts to her champagne glass with a wink, "Well then, we'd better get him back."

Damn right I'm getting him back. It's like fate has woven her web, tying our strings together. The company never said I had to bid on a girl, just a date. I suddenly want a date from this auction more than I've ever wanted anything, and I want it with Julian. If I have to throw down with an old lady to make that happen, I don't care.

"Up next is Julian!" the auctioneer says with a cheer, waving her hand for him to step up. He steps up from the line hesitantly. "Julian is a writer! Who here wants to be a part of Julian's romantic story? Let's start the bidding for this handsome man at two hundred dollars!"

My eyes dart around the room as hands shoot into the air. Ten freaking people have raised their paddles for him. Before I know it, the bids have reached five hundred dollars.

"Seven hundred dollars?" the auctioneer ventures coyly.

Readying myself, I take a deep breath and hold my paddle up high.

"Seven hundred dollars to the man in the corner!" she says excitedly, pointing in my direction. "Let's keep it going!" she adds into the microphone. "Do I hear eight hundred dollars?"

Before I can put my hand up, an older woman across the room lifts hers at a ridiculously fast speed, beating my bid. I scowl in her direction. Jesus, she's spry.

Game on old bat. *Game on.*

"Eight hundred to the lovely lady with the red hat!" the auctioneer chimes. "Can we get nine hundred?" She inquires.

Damn right she can get nine hundred. I shoot up my hand as fast as I can, glaring at the red hat lady across the room.

When my gaze darts to the stage, I finally meet Julian's. I can't decipher that expression on his face. Eyes wide, brows nearly to his hairline—is it happy befuddlement or sad befuddlement? I have no clue as to what his state of mind is, since he refuses to talk to me, but I'm determined to find out now. This man is going to talk to me. I'm winning this date, fair and square.

"Nine hundred to the gentleman in the corner! Do we have one thousand dollars?"

Before my hand can get in the air again, the red hat lady swings hers up again like she's committed to outbidding me. Ugh. She won't give up. She is not getting a date with *my man.*

"One thousand two hundred dollars?"

I leave my hand up and wave my paddle. I don't care about the price. He's mine.

"One thousand five hundred dollars?" The auctioneer queries, glancing back to the old lady.

So far, I'm five hundred dollars over my company's budget, but no amount of money will stop me.

I look back to Julian. His mouth is hanging open now, gawking at me. I looked away for too long though, ensnared by the eyes I've longed to see. The damn red hat lady just won the bid.

"Two thousand dollars?" the auctioneer suggests.

She's jumping the bid higher than she should, trying to get me for every penny she can. Shifting my hips, I stretch my arm higher.

"Going once for the gentlemen in the corner," she calls out with an amused smile.

I glare at red hat lady. She better fucking not.

"Going twice?" the auctioneer calls out again.

Yep, that's what I thought oldie. My arms are faster than yours.

"*Sold* to the gentlemen in the tuxedo for the generous price of two thousand dollars!" she cheers into the microphone.

I look around the room to inquiring eyes and slackened jaws. Without a second thought, I rise from my seat as Julian makes his way toward me. I take long strides, meeting him in the middle of the room. We're like two magnets, powerless against colliding.

"You're insane," he whispers when we're face to face. "You're insane, and I love you."

Grabbing his hands, I pull him into my chest, smashing my mouth against his. That's right. I'm making my statement. I don't give a fuck who sees us. I don't care what everyone at work thinks. I don't care what the world thinks.

Julian is mine, and I'm Julian's.

To my surprise, the room bursts into applause. I drown out the loud claps around me, immersing myself into the man whom I've been without, into the man I can never live without again.

He draws back, looking into my eyes, a smile on his face.

"I love you," I gasp, my heart pummeling the inside of my chest.

Taking his hand in mine, I turn around and face the room. My face feels beat red, and my heart is racing from all the attention we're getting, but I can't fight the biggest smile I've ever had. Looking around the room, it's full of people who look as ecstatic as I feel. Happy people. Accepting people.

Finding my table, I can see Mom and Oscar. They're clapping and cheering more boisterously than anyone else in the room. I give them an appreciative nod and then book it out of the banquet hall, hand in hand with Julian. *My Julian.*

JULES

CHAPTER 41

"I can't believe you told Oscar I was a woman," I say when we get outside the banquet hall.

I'm not mad at him anymore. How could I be after that stunt he just pulled inside, but I still need to give him a hard time. I mean, come on. I live with Nora for crying out loud. Harassment is second-nature.

Shit. I'm so damn happy it feels like I'm floating. I've been drowning in a sea of sadness, my world black and white until he showed up. When I'm with him, life is better. Everything is brighter, more alive. He's the man who made me live again. I didn't find love, it found me. Call it fate, call it destiny, maybe it was written in the stars. Maybe every single moment of my life was meant to lead up to this moment. I don't know, and I don't care.

"I just never corrected him when I found out you were a man," he explains. "And I'm so sorry for that," he adds.

THE RIGHT WRONG NUMBER

I lean against the brick wall behind me. Staring at him and crossing my arms over my chest, giving him an amused look. I go back to *Silicly 2001* like Nora suggested. I can understand the struggle all too well.

"Never again. *Never a-fucking-gain,*" he vows, taking my face in his hands. "I promise," he whispers.

I nod my head in agreement. "Is this fate, Liam? It feels like fate," I admit.

Whatever this is, it's undeniable. It's like the world is pushing us together, making us belong to each other.

Cocking his head to the side, he shrugs and laughs. "I don't know, but it looks like you're stuck with me."

He grabs my hand, intertwining our fingers together in a way that makes me sigh. His hand belongs in mine. It's where it's supposed to be.

I tug him toward me. "Since I'm stuck with you. Tell me, what are your plans for the future?" I smirk, bringing my face closer to his.

He draws his head back to look me in the eyes. We're inches from each other, our breath mixing, chests heaving.

"Waking up next to you," he whispers.

Good answer. Funny, the bed I forced myself to get out of is now the place I never want to leave again after hearing that.

"I'm so happy you weren't a serial killer," I whisper back before pressing our lips together, putting them exactly back where they belong.

Yes. I got two happily ever afters. I'm the luckiest man in the world.

EPILOGUE

Dear Diary,

It's been three-hundred-sixty-three days and approximately one of my lives since the happiest day of my lives.

The last time I wrote you, I was a very unhappy cat. I was what the humans call "temperamental." The humans in this house used to utter words such as *evil, beast,* and something about *Satan* at me during those dark days. I'm not sure what those terms mean, but whenever they yelled them, it sounded like they needed to hack up hairballs.

I decided to try harder to alleviate my dissatisfaction with my situation the day the man known as *Liam* walked into the door of my enclosure. As soon as I saw him, I knew he was going to be the one who turned my life around.

Lo and behold, a day came when Liam came into my enclosure and did not leave. He brought many new things into my enclosure, including a new couch that I made sure to mark with my scent so that he would know it met my approval. I would have normally been very despondent with such changes, and in return I would have gotten out my scratchers, but these changes were incredibly pleasing. If I could have jumped for joy, I would have.

There was a time when he did not come into my enclosure for over a week. It may have only been a week, but it felt like two of my lives had gone by. I have never been so depressed. I made sure to let the humans know how I felt about the dire situation. I marked my scent in places I knew they would not like. I knocked several cups off the counter. I went into the despicable human named Jules' room and destroyed all the papers on his desk with my scratchers.

I showed them!

I could not lose another acceptable human. Not again.

Diary, this is not all distressing though. On the contrary, my new human has come here to habituate permanently, and I could not be more pleased by the development. My favorite place is their bed, where I make my biscuits to show my new human my love. I settle right in between their bodies, reminding Jules that the human named Liam is mine. I cuddle close to him and he scritches my chin just right.

The happiest day of my life was when my new human figured out Tuna Tuesdays. My new human is smart, you see. I may have used my special mind powers on him to help him understand, but before I knew it, he cracked open that tuna can and I was chirping my special chirp again, the one that shows the humans when they have done something correctly.

I think about my old human from time to time. I miss his smell and the way he scratched behind my ears. He has been gone for many of my lives, but I will never forget him.

I'm still working on my new human, but with my mind melding powers, I will soon have him trained to be the perfect companion. Once I get this lady human who reeks of pureed grasses out of this house, I will have unsanctioned kibble.

Until then, I will hack up all my hairballs in her room and make sure to interrupt her nap times to nudge her along. She must go. Unsanctioned kibble, here I come.

After that, the only remaining disturbance is to get the human named Jules to stop doing things to get my new human to punish him in their bed. The disturbing moaning that human makes when my human is disciplining him is the stuff of nightmares. How is a respectable feline supposed to sleep with that kind of noise?

Fear not, Diary. Fishsticks will prevail, as always.

DR. THEO

If you'd like to read more about Dr. Theo, look for him in the *Sparrow's Nest* novels: *Rock Me Gently* and *Loving Out Loud,* by Dianna Roman and Katie Warren.

ACKNOWLEDGEMENTS

Thank you to these fine ass bitches who made this book what it is:

Dianna—for adding all the emotional shit, because I have a cold, dead heart. This book would have never happened if you didn't exist.

Jar and Chelsey—for reading this when it was still an atrocity.

To my tattoo artist, Govina —you nailed this cover.

To all my ARC readers who had faith in this book when they shouldn't have—y'all rock.

A special thanks to the ARC readers who offered to proofread this bad boy for me. Thanks for going through my mess.

I know none of y'all can see it, but I'm doing a happy dance right now. It's good. Like a million dollars good, and it's all because of your help. This dance is in your honor, and if you could see it, you'd feel more honored than you ever have before. Or you'd cringe and walk away. Whatever.

ABOUT THE AUTHOR

Katie lives in that thing called a *state* and rumor has it, in an underground bunker. She has a husband, one of those kid things, and some animals that arrived and never left. She tells her family, "I do what I want," on a frequent basis and suggests that you do the same. You can find her over in *the Bookstagram* world as @katieiscompletelyfine.

Printed in Great Britain
by Amazon